THE SAINT AND THE SINNER

Pandora was not eavesdropping. It was only by accident that she found herself overhearing the horrifying conversation between her uncle and guardian—the Bishop of Lindchester—and his wife.

"I have not had a chance to tell you," began Pandora's uncle, "that Prosper Witheridge asked me yesterday if he could pay his addresses to Pandora."

"You mean to say he wishes to marry her?" asked the Bishop's wife. "She should be grateful, deeply grateful, that a good man should wish to make her his wife."

Pandora suddenly realised that she had been holding her breath for so long that she was now gasping for air.

Prosper Witheridge! Was it possible for one moment to entertain the idea of him as a husband?

BARBARA CARTLAND

Bantam Books by Barbara Cartland
Ask your bookseller for the books you have missed

1	The Daring Deception	48	Conquered by Love
4	Lessons in Love	49	Never Laugh at Love
6	The Bored Bridegroom	50	The Secret of the Glen
8	The Dangerous Dandy	51	The Proud Princess
9	The Ruthless Rake	52	Hungry for Love
10	The Wicked Marquis	53	The Heart Triumphant
11	The Castle of Fear	54	The Dream and the Glory
13	A Sword to the Heart	55	The Taming of Lady
14	The Karma of Love		Lorinda
16	Bewitched	56	The Disgraceful Duke
18	The Frightened Bride	57	Vote for Love
19	The Shadow of Sin	59	The Magic of Love
21	The Tears of Love	60	Kiss the Moonlight
22	A Very Naughty Angel	61	A Rhapsody of Love
23	Call of the Heart	62	The Marquis Who Hated
24	The Devil in Love		Women
25	As Eagles Fly	63	Look, Listen and Love
26	Love Is Innocent	64	A Duel with Destiny
27	Say Yes, Samantha	65	The Curse of the Clan
28	The Cruel Count	66	Punishment of a Vixen
29	The Mask of Love	67	The Outrageous Lady
30	Blood on the Snow	68	A Touch of Love
31	An Arrow of Love	69	The Dragon and the
32	A Gamble with Hearts		Pearl
33	A Kiss for the King	70	The Love Pirate
34	A Frame of Dreams	71	The Temptation of
35	The Fragrant Flower		Torilla
36	The Elusive Earl	72	Love and the Loathsome
37	Moon over Eden		Leopard
38	The Golden Illusion	73	The Naked Battle
41	Passions in the Sand	74	The Hell-Cat and the
42	The Slaves of Love		King
43	An Angel in Hell	75	No Escape from Love
44	The Wild Cry of Love	76	The Castle Made for
45	The Blue-Eyed Witch		Love
46	The Incredible	77	The Sign of Love
	Honeymoon	78	The Saint and the Sinner
47	A Dream from the Night		

Barbara Cartland's Library of Love

1	The Sheik	7	The Way of an Eagle
2	His Hour	8	The Vicissitudes of
3	The Knave of		Evangeline
	Diamonds	9	The Bars of Iron
4	A Safety Match	10	Man and Maid
5	The Hundredth Chance	11	The Sons of the Sheik
6	The Reason Why	12	Six Days

Barbara Cartland
The Saint and the Sinner

BANTAM BOOKS
TORONTO · NEW YORK · LONDON

THE SAINT AND THE SINNER
Bantam edition | January 1978

ISBN 0–553–11395–2

Published simultaneously in the United States and Canada

Bantam Books are published by Bantam Books, Inc. Its trade-
mark, consisting of the words "Bantam Books" and the por-
trayal of a bantam, is registered in the United States Patent
Office and in other countries. Marca Registrada. Bantam
Books, Inc., 666 Fifth Avenue, New York, New York 10019.

PRINTED IN THE UNITED STATES OF AMERICA

Author's Note

John Milton, who ranks next to Shakespeare among English poets, published his epic *Paradise Lost* in 1667. The first edition was ten volumes.

With the fall of man as his theme, his brilliant, imaginative powers portrayed the conflict between good and evil, the contrast between Heaven and Hell, light and darkness, order and chaos.

Paradise Regained, published in 1671, was the logical sequence, since in it Christ, as the second Adam, won back from man what the first Adam lost.

Milton was eventually able to conquer despair and his later poems show a purified faith in God and in the regenerative strength of the individual Soul.

In 1820 Madame Vestris wore male attire when she played the Rake in a burlesque version of Mozart's *Don Giovanni* at Drury Lane. Many people were extremely shocked but the multitudes flocked to see her.

Next, as "Captain Macheath" in *The Beggar's Opera,* she was in breeches a fantastic draw.

Chapter One

1819

Pandora sewed the cover that she had washed and pressed back onto the cushion, thinking as she did so that it would be hard to choose a more hideous colour or design.

It was a kind of "liver" brown and the embroidery on it was a sickly shade of green.

Her father had so often said that people could be associated with colours, and she thought that these were typical of her Aunt Sophie.

She gave a little sigh as she thought of how unhappy she had been since she had come to live in the Bishop's Palace at Lindchester.

It was large, oppressive, cold, and in Pandora's eyes excessively ugly. That was the word, she decided, that described her life ever since she had arrived there.

She had been so happy in the small Vicarage at Chart with its rose-filled gardens and the stables which held her father's horses—the horses which her mother had often said with a laugh were the most important members of the family.

Her father had never really wished to be a Parson, but then being the third son in a family dedicated to the Church, he had really had little choice.

However, he had been clever enough to obtain a

living where there was little to do and he could ride and hunt to his heart's content.

"The Hunting Parson" they called him, but more often than not they forgot that he preached on Sunday and instead thought of him just as an attractive, jovial man who was the friend of everyone in the hunting-field and everywhere else.

What fun it had been just being in his company, Pandora thought, and forced back the tears that immediately misted her eyes.

She had cried so desperately and uncontrollably, when she had first learnt of the accident that had killed her father and mother, that she thought afterwards she had no tears left.

And yet, after more than a year of living with her uncle, the Bishop of Lindchester, she found it increasingly difficult not to cry, because everything seemed so bleak and she was so desperately alone.

Even now she could not bear to think of the accident which had taken her father and mother from her.

Because her father could not afford well-trained horses he usually broke them in himself.

He was trying out a pair that were still rather wild when he and his wife were enjoying a day's hunting on the other side of the County.

The day before they were to ride, Charles Stratton had sent the two horses to a stable belonging to a friend, so that they would be fresh when he and his wife arrived in the gig in which he always travelled.

It was old and, as he admitted, somewhat rickety, but it carried him where he wished to go and that was all that mattered.

He left the gig and the horses which drew it in the stable which had housed the hunters and they had a glorious day with a long run, which was what Charles Stratton enjoyed more than anything else.

Both he and his wife were tired when as dusk was falling they set off home along the narrow lanes which led eventually to Chart.

It had been a crisp, bright day, but now there

was undoubtedly a sharp frost and Charles Stratton said somewhat ruefully:

"It looks as if we shall not be able to hunt for the rest of the week."

"It may turn to snow," his wife replied optimistically.

"I doubt it," he said. "Are you warm enough, my darling?"

"Quite warm, thank you," she answered, nestling a little closer to him.

They reached the top of a long hill which led down to a river, and Charles Stratton realised that there was ice on the road and he would have to drive carefully.

He reined in his horses, and was proceeding more slowly when suddenly a stag leapt over a fence in front of them and rushed across the road only a yard or so ahead.

It terrified the horses, which broke into a wild and uncontrollable gallop, and in a moment they were hurtling at a breakneck pace towards the river.

Pandora had been told exactly what happened: the old gig had smashed against the bridge and her father and mother had been thrown down a steep embankment and into the river itself.

Her father's neck had been broken, while her mother, knocked unconscious, had fallen face downwards into the water and drowned.

Pandora often wished that she had been with them and that she too had died.

When her uncle, the Bishop, had with obvious reluctance and a great deal of hypocritical magnanimity taken her to live with him and his wife in the Palace, she had thought it would be impossible ever to laugh again.

Certainly there was nothing to laugh about in the company of her uncle and aunt.

They were not physically cruel to her but they obviously resented her presence, and everything she did was wrong in their eyes.

It was impossible to please them, however hard

she tried, and after a while, because she was intelligent, she realised that it was her looks that offended her aunt more than anything else.

She was very like her mother, and her heart-shaped face and large pansy-coloured eyes were such a contrast to her aunt's overblown figure and lined face that she could in fact understand why the older woman resented her.

There were always innumerable tasks for her to do, and although she was prepared to do them willingly, the results were never precisely what her aunt wanted.

Now she was quite sure that there would be something wrong with the cushion: she would have sewn it too tightly or too loosely, or it would not have been pressed to her aunt's satisfaction, and there was every likelihood of her having to do it all over again.

Then with a sigh of relief she realised that her uncle and aunt were leaving at noon for London.

They had been invited to the garden-party to be given by the Bishop of London at Lambeth Palace.

It was an event which her aunt looked forward to year after year, and for three weeks Pandora had been altering her gown, including adding extra lace, refurbishing her bonnet, and doing innumerable renovations to the sunshade she would carry.

Whatever Aunt Sophie wore, with her stout figure she would look ungainly, and that was undoubtedly one of the reasons why at breakfast she looked with distinct animosity at Pandora's slender figure, which could not be disguised by the plain, almost Puritan-like gown she was wearing.

It had been the usual silent meal because the Bishop did not like talking early in the morning.

Instead, he read *The Times*, propped up in front of him on a silver holder that was polished assiduously by the Butler.

Two footmen handed round a large amount of food in silver dishes from which Augustus Stratton and his wife reinforced themselves for the journey which lay ahead.

Pandora ate very little and was relieved when her aunt gave her three lists on closely written sheets of paper.

"These are the things you are to do while I am away, Pandora," she said in her hard voice. "There is no need to be slack and indolent because your uncle and I are not here. You will tick off each thing as you do it, and I shall expect every item to be completed before I return on Friday."

"I will do my best, Aunt Sophie."

"Then let us hope that your best is better than it usually is!" her aunt said scathingly.

Pandora took the lists, rose from the table, curt-seyed, and left the room.

Once she had closed the door, she ran to the small Sitting-Room where she kept her sewing-basket and other personal things.

But instead of reading the lists as she should have done, she went to the window to look out at the sunshine and thought with a feeling of joy that she was free!

Free for three days of fault-finding and grumbling, of veiled innuendos about her father and mother, and of undisguised criticisms of herself and her appearance.

"What shall I do? How shall I spend the time?" she asked, and knew the answer.

As soon as her uncle and aunt had left, she would ride over to Chart and talk to the villagers there who had loved her father and mother.

She would not go to the Vicarage, for she could not bear to see other people living in what she still thought of as her home.

But there were others who would welcome her gladly because she was her father's daughter and because they had known her ever since she was a small child.

She put the cushion back onto the chair on which it belonged and thought again how ugly it was.

As she did so, the door by the fireplace in the corner of the room gave a little click and she realised it had blown open because someone had entered her uncle's Study, which was next door.

Then she heard her aunt's voice.

"Before we leave, Augustus, you will tell Pandora that she is not to go riding near Chart Hall."

"I was just thinking of Pandora," her uncle replied. "I have not had a chance to tell you, Sophie, that yesterday, before he left to visit his father, Prosper Witheridge asked me if he could pay his addresses to her."

"You mean to say he wishes to marry Pandora?" Mrs. Stratton asked, as if such an unlikely idea had never crossed her mind.

"He says he has a deep regard for her," the Bishop replied, "but, quite rightly, he has not spoken to her but instead has asked my permission to do so."

"Then all I can say is that I should have thought he had more sense," Mrs. Stratton said sharply. "But of course, as far as your niece is concerned she should be grateful, deeply grateful, that a good man should wish to make her his wife."

"Pandora is very young," the Bishop said reflectively. "I should have thought it better if she waited awhile before taking on the responsibility of marriage."

"She will never get a better offer," Mrs. Stratton said. "Of course, Lord Witshaw has two older sons, but nevertheless Prosper is an 'Honourable' and that amounts to something—in fact a great deal!"

"I was not particularly thinking of the Social World's side," the Bishop said.

"Then what else?" his wife asked quickly.

There was a pause before she added:

"How can you possibly hesitate in giving permission, if that is what you have done?"

"I told him I would think about it," the Bishop answered, "and let him know my decision on our return from London."

"Then it will be 'yes,' Augustus, an unequivocal 'yes'! For I assure you it will be a great relief for me to have Pandora off our hands. I only hope that

Prosper Witheridge is strong enough to curb that regrettably wild streak in her, which undoubtedly she inherited from her mother's family—not yours."

Again there was silence until Mrs. Stratton said:

"That reminds me, I was telling you why you must forbid Pandora to go to Chart. That man is in residence, I believe."

"The Earl?"

"Who else? I was told that His Lordship arrived two days ago, and you know as well as I do what that means."

"I do indeed!" the Bishop said heavily. "And there is nothing I can do about it after the way he spoke to me when I remonstrated with him."

"He is a disgrace to his name and to the neighbourhood," Mrs. Stratton said positively, "and Lindchester will be agog with stories of what is taking place at Chart Hall and the people who are staying there."

She made a sound that was one of disgust combined with irritation.

"Lady Henderson tells me," she continued, lowering her voice, "that the women whom the Earl entertains are nothing but doxies and play-actresses. No decent man would be seen in the company of such creatures!"

"Lady Henderson," the Bishop retorted, "should not soil her lips by speaking of the dregs of the London sewers! And I hope, Sophie, that you will not encourage those who spread tales of what happens at Chart Hall. You know as well as I do that stories are often exaggerated and only harm those who listen to them."

"It would be difficult to exaggerate anything that was said about the Earl," Mrs. Stratton replied. "You are to forbid Pandora from going anywhere near the village. She is more likely to obey you than me."

"I will tell her," the Bishop replied, "and Prosper Witheridge, who will be returning tonight, can doubtless keep an eye on her."

"The less he hears about Pandora's relatives, the

better! It might make him think twice about his offer of marriage," Mrs. Stratton said spitefully, and Pandora heard the door of the Study close behind her.

She had stood without moving as she had listened to what was being said in the next room.

Now she heard the heavy footsteps of her uncle moving about as if he was collecting various papers, and then the Study door opened and closed again.

Pandora realised that she had been holding her breath for so long now that she was almost gasping for air.

Prosper Witheridge! Was it possible for one moment to entertain the idea of him as a husband?

He had been her uncle's Chaplain for only three months, and because instinctively she had sensed that the way in which he looked at her was not that of a man dedicated to the Service of God, she had avoided him on every possible occasion.

But now, if her aunt had her way, she was to marry him!

She was well aware that as she was only eighteen and her uncle was her Guardian, it would be very difficult for her to oppose any decision he made about her future.

But, Prosper Witheridge!

Even to think of him made her feel as if her skin crawled, and as her father would have said jokingly: "There's a goose walking over your grave!"

"I cannot marry him . . . I cannot!" she said aloud. "I hate him! There is something about him which makes me feel . . . revolted in a way I have never felt about any other man!"

But she knew that once her uncle had given his blessing to the betrothal, it would be very difficult, if not impossible, for her to say or do anything to prevent the marriage from taking place.

"I hate him! I hate him!" she said again.

Then she shivered as she thought of the look in Prosper Witheridge's eyes and of how his hands always seemed to be hot and clammy.

She felt suddenly as if the Palace was a prison

in which she was incarcerated, and if she left it as Prosper Witheridge's wife she knew that it would be to exchange a large prison for a smaller one, and she would never be free again.

"I cannot bear it!" she whispered beneath her breath.

Then she heard her aunt calling for her.

She ran across the room and into the hall to find that her uncle and aunt were ready to depart, the servants carrying their luggage outside to the travelling-coach.

"Where have you been, you tiresome girl?" Mrs. Stratton asked. "You are never there when you are wanted. You knew perfectly well that your uncle and I were leaving at half after ten."

"I am sorry, Aunt Sophie, I forgot the time," Pandora said meekly.

"Forgot! Forgot! That is all you ever do! As I have told you before, your head is full of holes. Now kindly behave yourself while we are away. Mrs. Norris will be coming over to sleep in the Palace at night, but she cannot be here before six o'clock in the evening, so you will have to look after yourself until she arrives."

"Yes, Aunt Sophie."

"Your uncle has something to say to you," Mrs. Stratton said with a meaningful glance at her husband.

"Yes, yes, of course," the Bishop said, as if he had forgotten what he had been told to say to his niece. "You are not, Pandora, to go riding anywhere near Chart Hall before we return. Is that understood?"

"Yes, Uncle Augustus."

"Then kindly remember what your uncle has said to you," Mrs. Stratton said sharply. "If you disobey him, Pandora, you will be severely punished when we return."

"Yes, Aunt Sophie."

Mrs. Stratton swept to the front door and down the steps to the Bishop's travelling-carriage.

It was a very impressive vehicle with his coat-of-arms emblazoned on the panel of each door and the coachman and footman dressed in the livery of his ecclesiastical rank. There were four out-riders to accompany them on the journey to London.

As the Bishop went down the steps with Pandora beside him, he said quietly:

"Try to please your aunt, my child, and do not get into any mischief while we are away from home."

"I will try, Uncle Augustus."

For a moment the Bishop's eyes rested on his niece as if he appreciated the sunshine glinting on her fair hair and in her pansy-coloured eyes.

Then a voice from inside the carriage said peremptorily:

"Augustus! We should be on our way."

"Yes, of course, my dear."

The Bishop stepped in, a footman shut the door of the carriage, and the cavalcade started off in a manner which, Pandora thought, should have been heralded with a fanfare of trumpets.

She watched them drive out of the court-yard and onto the short drive which led to the highway, and then she turned and went back into the Palace.

They had gone!

She was free, and yet any elation she might have felt was overshadowed by what she had just heard her uncle say.

Not realising where her feet were carrying her, she walked into her uncle's Study.

It would have been a pleasant room if her aunt had not furnished it with mustard-coloured curtains and a carpet in which the same colour predominated, intermingled with various shades of brown.

The room looked austere with no flowers, no touches of colour to relieve the sombreness of it.

Yet the arm-chairs were well upholstered—for the Bishop liked his comfort—and his large desk was piled with papers, all of them neatly arranged.

Pandora had the idea that she was filed in a

category headed: "Pandora Stratton—Niece and Object of Charity."

'If I had any money,' she thought, 'I would go to London and find myself some employment and make myself independent.'

It was an idea so revolutionary, so impractical, that she might just as well have thought of flying to the moon or living beneath the sea.

The very little money her father had left had been taken over by her uncle, and she presumed it would be used for her trousseau and to provide a dowry for her marriage.

Her marriage!

Again the idea seemed to strike at her as if it were a knife.

"What can I do? Oh, Papa, what can I do?" she asked aloud.

She knew that her father and mother would never have forced her into marriage with a man she did not like.

They had married in defiance of the Chart family, which had been horrified that one of their members should wish to marry someone so penniless and, to their minds, so unimportant as a Parson.

But when they met Charles Stratton, a number of them, Lady Eveline later told her daughter, had understood.

"Your father was such a handsome, attractive, and happy person," she said. "I think my aunts, my cousins, and even grandmother, all of whom had disapproved, almost fell in love with him themselves!"

That was not to say, Pandora knew, that they would have sacrificed their important position in the Social World as her mother had done to live in a small Vicarage, and be, with very little money, supremely happy.

"Have you ever regretted marrying Papa?" Pandora had asked once.

Her mother laughed.

"Do I look as if I ever regretted being the happiest woman in the world?" she asked. "I adore your father and he adores me, and, what is more, we have an adorable daughter! Could any woman ask for more?"

It had certainly never seemed to worry her mother that she could not do the things she had done when she was a girl.

There was no question of going to London to Balls and parties in the Season or of accepting the invitations she occasionally received from the Prince Regent at Carlton House.

Instead, she was quite content to make the small Vicarage comfortable and attractive for her husband, and to skimp and save on everything else so that they could afford to ride together in the summer and go hunting in the winter.

It somehow did not seem incongruous that the horses which Charles Stratton had prized so much should have been responsible for his tragic death.

Pandora even in her grief sometimes thought it better that her father and mother had died together, because either would have been completely lost without the other.

That was the sort of marriage she wanted for herself, so how, having seen two people so happy, so content with each other, could she contemplate being married to someone like Prosper Witheridge?

It was not only that she shrank from him physically; he was also pompous, sanctimonious, and ready to criticise and find fault with everything, just like her aunt.

Her father had been extremely tolerant of the failings of others.

"They do their best," he would say when someone was criticised, or: "We must give them a chance. People can only give what they are capable of giving, and often we ask too much."

Prosper Witheridge would never think like that, and Pandora knew that he would have a great deal to say about the party that was taking place at Chart Hall.

Nobody in the Bishop's Palace ever thought how much it hurt her to hear them disparaging the man who was her cousin.

He might be all they said he was, but she thought it would have been tactful if they had kept their condemnation of him until she was not present.

She had never met the present Earl of Chartwood because her grandfather, the fourth Earl, had died two months after the death of her father and mother.

He had been old and ailing for some time, and, as was to be expected, Pandora knew that he had hated his heir presumptive ferociously and had never allowed him to come to Chart Hall.

It was understandable because her mother's two brothers had both been killed in the war.

The youngest had been a sailor, killed when he was only sixteen at the Battle of the Nile, fighting with Nelson in his magnificent victory over the French fleet.

The elder son, of whom Pandora had been very fond, had been killed at Waterloo.

Their father had been stricken not only at losing them but in knowing that the title and the Estate must now go to an obscure cousin in whom he had never taken any interest.

It had seemed that the succession was assured, but then suddenly his sons had been swept away from him and then his daughter had died.

As one of the villagers had said to Pandora:

"When your mother went, His Lordship just turned his face to the wall and there was no heart left in him."

Pandora could understand because she felt the same, but it had been painful to learn that the fifth Earl of Chartwood was a very different man from what her uncles had been.

Stories soon reached Lindchester of his extravagances, of wild parties, of huge wagers laid on horses, of behaviour that was apparently so outrageous that people only whispered about it in Pandora's presence.

Then, soon after his succession, the new Earl had come to Chart Hall and Pandora had hoped a little wistfully that he might invite her to meet him.

There were plenty of people both in the house and on the Estate to tell him where she had gone to live, but instead there were stories at Christmastime of what amounted to an orgy.

It had kept the gossips of the Cathedral town chattering like an aviary of parrots.

They talked of little else until he came for the second time, two months later. Then it appeared that the County families who had intended to call were too scandalised to do so.

When Pandora spoke to people in the village, they talked of changes and of the Earl himself with fear in their eyes.

Her aunt denounced him in no uncertain terms, and Pandora learnt that her uncle had called formally, not only to make the new Earl's acquaintance but also to remonstrate with him about certain things that were being done on the Estate.

He came back both angry and affronted.

"It is a long time since I have been insulted in such a manner!" he said.

But he would not relate exactly what had happened, except, Pandora gathered, that the Earl had made a mockery of everything her uncle revered.

It was now June and Pandora guessed that the Regent would have left London for Brighton and the leaders of Society would have followed him.

Therefore, the Earl of Chartwood had, like most of his friends, moved from his town house to his country Estate.

There was no doubt that his arrival would result in the same excitement in Lindchester. The gossips would be waiting for each tit-bit of scandal that they could repeat and rerepeat to each other over the tea-tables.

Pandora knew it would hurt her because in disparaging the Earl she felt as if they also disparaged the name that had been her mother's.

The Chart family had been playing their part in the history of England for centuries.

There had been Charts who had been Royalists at the time of Charles I, Charts who had fought with the Duke of Marlborough at Blenheim, Charts who had played their part in India and in other parts of the world.

It was to Pandora as if their blood in her cried out against the new Earl being subjected to the slings and arrows of the petty, unimportant little people of Lindchester, who really delighted in being in a position to defame him.

"I wonder what he is really like?" she said to herself.

Then suddenly an idea came to her, an idea so fantastic that for a moment she almost laughed as she thought of it.

And yet quite clearly she could hear her aunt saying in this very room:

"The Earl entertains nothing but doxies and play-actresses. No decent man would be seen in the company of such creatures!"

No decent man . . .

The words seemed to burn themselves into Pandora's mind, and suddenly it seemed to her as if here was a way out, here was a way of escape.

She walked to the window and stood looking with unseeing eyes at the trimmed garden, so neat with its flower-beds and clipped yews that she almost felt there was something unnatural about it.

She had a sudden vision of the green velvet lawns at Chart, of the herb-garden enclosed by its Elizabethan walls, of the rose-garden fragrant and vivid with colour surrounding an ancient sun-dial.

She felt home-sick for it in a manner that was almost a physical ache in her heart and in her mind.

Then the same idea presented itself again to her so clearly, so precisely, that it was almost like looking at the pieces of a puzzle falling into place and the answer was there.

She sat down at her uncle's desk, something she

would never have dared to do if he had been at home, and wrote a letter on the thick vellum paper that was kept entirely for him.

Then, having folded it, she fastened it with a wafer and went upstairs to the small room she had been allotted on the second floor of the Palace.

She rang the bell for a maid and when one came she gave her instructions in a quiet, calm voice which almost surprised herself.

*   *   *

An hour later Pandora was driving away from the Palace in one of the carriages which she and her aunt used when they went calling at the houses in the vicinity of Lindchester.

The old coachman looked surprised when she directed him to where she wished to go, but he had been too long in the service of the Bishop to query any order he was given.

Pandora sitting back in the open carriage was conscious that a small trunk containing her clothes was strapped on behind.

They crossed the river by the ancient bridge which had first been built in Norman times.

Then they were in the open countryside with its green trees, fields ripening with corn, and beyond them woods which made excellent cover in the winter for those who hunted there.

Pandora had not been allowed to go hunting since coming to live with her uncle. One of her father's horses had been kept for her to ride, but the rest had been sold.

She knew it was a concession to have even one, and her aunt's most frequent threat when she was annoyed was to say that she would take away from her the privilege of being allowed to ride.

She could not help thinking with a slight smile of amusement that in driving to Chart she was obeying her uncle in the letter if not the spirit of his order.

She had been told not to ride in the vicinity of

Chart Hall. Well, she was not—she was driving there.

She told herself that if her expedition failed and she returned ignominiously, no-one would know except the servants, and because they liked her and disliked her aunt it was doubtful that they would betray her.

She had now driven over three miles outside the town and was in the quiet, beautiful countryside which she had known all her life.

The woods were much thicker here, and she remembered how she had loved roaming in them as a child and riding in them when she was older.

There were streams winding through meadowland and one where her father occasionally went fishing and caught fat, brown trout which they enjoyed for breakfast.

There were memories every inch of the way. Then at last they came to the village with its black and white cottages with their thatched roofs.

All the gardens were bright with flowers and Pandora remembered that it was her mother's idea to give a prize for the best garden every year, so that the local people strove to make their village the most beautiful in the whole County.

Pandora knew the inhabitants of every cottage they passed, but at this time of the day the men would be out working in the fields and many of the women would be working at the Castle.

In her grandfather's time they had been employed in the kitchens, the laundry, and the dairy.

She wondered if there were still the big wide bowls of thick cream standing on the stone slabs waiting to be made into the golden pats of butter that were stamped with the Chart crest.

She had loved to watch the dairymaids at work and sometimes she would ask if she could help, but soon found it very tiring to turn the cream in the churn until it became butter.

Now the Castle was in sight.

It always looked magnificent at any time of the

year, but perhaps most of all in the summer when it was surrounded with green trees as if it were a precious jewel.

The grey stone glowed against the trees, and the chimneys, statues, and urns on the roof were silhouetted against the sky.

It had a majesty and an importance that spoke without words of the great family it housed.

Every generation of the Chart family had added to the original building, which had been commenced in the reign of Queen Elizabeth.

The second Earl, however, who, having been impressed with houses like Blenheim, Hatfield, and Burleigh, had employed Inigo Jones to improve Chart Hall.

He had added two wings and a new facade, making it an outstanding edifice as well as a beautiful one.

"I love Chart!" Pandora exclaimed.

It was part of her life.

There was the lake where her father had taken her boating amongst the water-lilies, the lawns where she had rolled down their slopes when she was a small child, screaming with excitement.

At the back of the house there were the shrubberies where she had played hide-and-seek and the greenhouses from which the old gardener had given her peaches so large that she could hardly hold them in her small hands.

'If only Uncle George had not been killed at Waterloo,' she thought wistfully.

He had been very like her mother and he would never have allowed her to live with her father's relatives, who did not like her.

The carriage drew up outside the long flight of steps leading to the front door.

A footman, whom Pandora did not recognise, came hurrying down the steps to open the door of the carriage and Pandora stepped out.

It was like coming home, she thought, to walk into the huge cool hall with its statues of Grecian goddesses set in alcoves, while the ceiling, painted by an Italian master, rioted with colour.

A strange Butler with a somewhat supercilious expression on his face stood waiting for her to speak.

"I wish to see the Earl of Chartwood," Pandora said.

It disconcerted her to find that she did not know the servants. She had expected old Burrows to be there and the footmen who had once been boys in the village and had sung in the choir.

The Butler did not ask her name but gave her what she thought was a disdainful glance before he walked across the hall and opened the door to the Morning-Room.

It was a room that her grandfather had liked because it had a view over the gardens and it was smaller than the grand Salons and therefore more easy to keep warm in the winters.

Pandora waited, but to her surprise the Butler went into the room, leaving her outside.

She heard him say:

"There's a lady to see you, M'Lord."

"Another?" a voice answered. "Good God, Dalton, who can it be now?"

"I've no idea, M'Lord."

"Another little bee to flutter round the honeypot, I presume. They smell it, that is what they do, Dalton, they smell out the honey, wherever it may be."

"As you say, M'Lord."

"Well, show her in, but God knows I did not invite her."

The Butler returned to Pandora's side, where she stood, still astonished and a little shocked by what she had heard.

Too late she wished she had not come, but now there was nothing for it but to obey the almost imperious gesture which the Butler made for her to enter.

She walked into the room, instinctively straightening her back and lifting her chin a little.

A quick glance told her that nothing had been changed since her grandfather's time.

The three long windows admitted the sunshine and for a moment it dazzled her eyes so that it was hard to find the only occupant of the room.

Then she saw him.

He was lounging in a high-backed chair that her grandfather had invariably used, with one leg over the arm, the other stretched out in front of him.

He held a glass in his hand and for a moment Pandora found it difficult to focus her eyes on his face.

Then she saw that he was undoubtedly a Chart, with the same pansy-coloured eyes as her own, except for the fact that his were darker and harder, and his eye-brows, which were dark like his hair, almost met across his nose.

There were fair Charts and dark Charts and the dark ones were those who were dangerous and also adventurous.

"Your hair's the wrong colour, that's what's wrong about you!" her Nanny had often said when she had done something particularly naughty. "You're meant to be good with your fair hair, and don't you forget it!"

The new Earl was very dark and his hair had an almost Byronesque look to it, an impression that was accentuated by the fact that he had pulled loose his cravat and it hung untidily down the front of his shirt.

He had been riding, Pandora noticed, for he was not only in riding-breeches but his highly polished boots were covered in dust.

She stood looking at him, hardly aware that she was staring. Then he said in what was a jeering, mocking voice:

"Well, who are you and what do you want?"

Rather belatedly, because she had been so interested in what she saw, Pandora curtseyed.

"I am your cousin, Pandora Stratton," she replied, "and I have come here to ask for your . . . help."

He looked at her in astonishment although he made no attempt to rise.

"Pandora Stratton," he repeated. "And you say you are my cousin?"

"Not a very close one, but the late Earl was my grandfather."

The Earl pushed back his head and laughed.

"Your grandfather? Well, thank God you are not like him, but I am certainly surprised to see you, Cousin Pandora. I understood I was to be ostracised by all my relations."

"Are you?" Pandora enquired. "I did not know."

"You must be very out-of-touch," the Earl replied with a sneer. Then he said: "No, of course! I know! Stratton—you are something to do with that sanctimonious, psalm-singing Bishop who called on me last time I was here."

"He is . . . my uncle."

"Then all I can say is that I am sorry for you!"

"I am rather sorry for . . . myself."

He smiled for the first time and it made his face look quite different.

"I suppose you want to tell me about it," he said, "but if you are asking me to subscribe to the poor, the diseased, the crippled, or the out of work in Lindchester, you can save your breath!"

"I am not asking for help for any of them," Pandora replied, "although doubtless they would appreciate it . . . but for . . . myself."

She seated herself as she spoke in a chair opposite the Earl.

He stared at her, taking in, she thought, every detail of her plain, unornamented gown, her bonnet decorated only with the ribbons with which it was tied under her chin.

"I suppose you have some resemblance to all those toffee-nosed ancestors who bedeck the walls here," he said.

"As I expect you know, there are fair Charts and dark Charts," Pandora said. "You represent one and I the other."

"What is the difference?"

"One is good and the other is bad."

The Earl laughed again.

"Well, that makes things simple, at any rate, and I do my best to live up to what is expected of me. Now—you say you need my help? What can have occurred to bring the Saint to the Sinner?"

Now Pandora laughed because she could not help it. Then she said quite seriously:

"I have come to see you, Cousin Norvin, because you are the only person ... I think, who can ... save me."

"I only hope you are not talking about your soul," the Earl remarked.

"I am talking about my life ... or rather ... my future," Pandora answered. "You see, my uncle, the Bishop, intends that I should ... marry his Chaplain, the Honourable Prosper Witheridge."

"And what am I expected to do about it?" the Earl asked bluntly.

Pandora suddenly felt shy and her eyes dropped. After a moment she said in a very small voice:

"I wondered if you ... would ... ask me to ... stay here for ... a night ... or two."

After she had spoken there was silence. Then the Earl said:

"Am I hearing you aright? You are inviting yourself to stay with me because you think in some way, which I cannot imagine, it will prevent your marriage?"

There was a pause before he added:

"I must be very dense, but I cannot understand what your are suggesting."

Pandora drew in her breath.

"I hope what I ... say will ... not make you ... angry."

"Does it matter if it does?"

"It ... it might prevent you from being ... sympathetic and ... understanding."

"Two virtues which are lamentably lacking in

my make-up," the Earl replied. "But I would still like you to explain what you are trying to say."

Pandora drew in her breath.

"My uncle and aunt have gone to ... London to attend a garden-party at Lambeth Palace."

"I am sorry for them," the Earl said with a twist of his lips. "One Parson is enough at any time, but a conclave of them would undoubtedly try the patience of any Saint!"

Pandora smiled faintly, but she went on:

"Before they left I ... overheard my uncle say that his Chaplain had asked if he could pay his ... addresses to me. My aunt was ... insistent that my uncle should give his ... consent and that I should ... marry Mr. Witheridge."

"And you have no wish to do so?"

"He is horrible!" Pandora replied. "I dislike him and I would do anything in the world rather than ... become his wife."

"Even come to me for help!" the Earl said mockingly.

"I should have liked to meet you anyway," Pandora answered. "After all, you are living here in Chart, which I have known ever since I was a child. I love the Castle and I love the village, where I was brought up."

There was just a little throb in her voice which the Earl heard.

"Go on with your story," he said. "I still cannot see where I come into all this."

Pandora again looked embarrassed. Then with the colour rising in her face she said:

"My aunt said she had been ... told that the ... women you have ... staying here are nothing but doxies ... I am not sure what that means ... and play-actresses and no ... decent man would ... associate with them."

She dared not look at the Earl as she went on hesitatingly:

"I ... I thought that if I ... stayed here ... Mr.

Witheridge would not wish to . . . associate with me."

For a moment there was silence, then the Earl laughed uproariously.

He laughed until he coughed. Then for the first time he straightened himself in the chair and taking his leg from the arm of it he said:

"I follow your reasoning and, my God! is it a jest? A funnier one I have never heard—that you should come to me—me, of all people—to save you from the attentions of a Parson!"

He rose from the chair as he spoke and walked across the room to where there was a grog-tray. He filled his glass from a decanter and said:

"I fear I have been lamentably inhospitable in not offering you any refreshment. Is there anything you would like?"

"N-no . . . thank you."

Now Pandora looked at him and her eyes were very anxious in her pale face.

"You really want to do this outrageous thing?" the Earl asked, coming back to stand on the hearth-rug, his glass in his hand.

"There is . . . no other way," Pandora said earnestly. "You must see I am trapped. Uncle Augustus is my Guardian, and when Papa and Mama were killed . . . no-one else offered to have me to . . . live with them."

"What will happen if you simply say you will not marry this man you dislike so intensely?" the Earl asked, and now he was not jeering.

"They will . . . force me to do so," Pandora said in a low voice. "I do not think in law that I have any . . . choice, and my aunt . . . dislikes me and is anxious to be . . . rid of me."

She paused before she added:

"She is quite old, but I think, although it sounds conceited, that she is a little . . . jealous of me."

"That is not surprising."

The Earl drank from his glass before he added:

"There must be some alternative to what you are

suggesting. You realise what will be said about you if you stay here."

"Yes . . . I understand," Pandora said. "But . . . please, do let me stay . . . just for two nights. I am sure that after that Mr. Witheridge will change his mind. He is very conscious of his own . . . consequence, and he says that you have made this place a . . . house of sin!"

"Damn his impertinence!" the Earl said. "What can someone like him know about sin, and who is he to sit in judgement upon me?"

"You have certainly . . . scandalised the . . . neighbourhood."

"That is exactly what I meant to do."

His eyes narrowed and there was a sudden, hard line to his mouth.

"I wanted them to be shocked and horrified— and that includes my relatives—all of them, including you!"

There was a harsh note in his voice and what seemed to Pandora almost a cruel look in his eyes. Then he said:

"But of course! Why am I hesitating? Come and stay, little Pandora. Walk into my hornets' nest. Make yourself comfortable in the house of sin. I welcome you—I welcome you with open arms!"

"Do you really mean that?"

"Have I not told you I am prepared to be your host and invite you to be my guest for as long as you wish to stay? My house is yours!"

"Oh, thank you! Thank you!" Pandora cried. "Then do you think a servant could give this note to the coachmen and tell them to return to Lindchester without me?"

"What is it?" the Earl asked.

"It is a letter to Mr. Witheridge to tell him where I am."

"You have certainly thought of everything!"

"I tried to," Pandora answered. "He comes back tonight from having visited his father, and when he learns I am here I think he will be both ... horrified and ... disgusted!"

"I am sure he will be!" the Earl said, and there was a note of satisfaction in his voice.

"I have brought a trunk with me," Pandora said, "hoping that you would be kind enough to let me stay."

The Earl put out his hand to the bell-pull and almost immediately the door opened.

"Take this note to Miss Stratton's carriage and tell the coachmen to return home," he said. "Miss Stratton is staying, so bring in her trunk."

"Yes, M'Lord."

There was a look of surprise on the Butler's face which Pandora did not miss.

"I thought I should find Burrows here," she said. "Have you made many changes in the household?"

"I have no idea," the Earl replied. "I have an agent who attends to all that sort of thing."

Pandora knew that this was one of the reasons why the people in the village had been upset and frightened.

She was just about to say more when the door opened and into the room came one of the most beautiful women she had ever seen.

She had hair that was a brilliant red and her skin in contrast was so white that it took Pandora a second or two to realise that it was not natural.

Her lips were scarlet and she was wearing an inordinate amount of jewellery on a low-cut gown which concealed very little of her full, curved figure.

She seemed almost to float into the room and looked from Pandora to the Earl in a questioning manner that was somehow offensive.

"I heard a *lady* had arrived!" she said, accentuating the word, "and wondered who it might be. I thought our guests were not expected until later."

"You need not get excited," the Earl replied. "This is my cousin, Pandora Stratton, whom I have never met before."

"You expect me to believe that?" the newcomer enquired.

She looked at Pandora in an even more suspicious manner than she had before.

Because she felt she must say something, Pandora explained quickly:

"I live in Lindchester and I came to ask my cousin for help."

"He's got no money for charity," the woman said rudely. "I see to that!"

"Shut up, Kitty, and behave yourself!" the Earl said. "My cousin has every right to ask my help if she wants it, and in fact she is not after money."

"Then what is she after?"

"Just an invitation to stay for a night or two because she thinks it will cool the ardour of a Parson who wishes to marry her."

The woman stared at him incredulously, then she laughed.

"God Almighty! What are we coming to?" she asked. "There isn't really a part in this play for you, Norvin, as you must be well aware."

"On the contrary, I am quite prepared to play the part of Stage Manager, or that of the villain," the Earl replied. "Now, suppose we start at the beginning and you are introduced?"

He made a gesture with his hand.

"Pandora, this is Kitty King, and as I fancy you have no knowledge of the London Theatre, let me tell you she plays an important part at Drury Lane and also understudies the famous Madame Vestris with great gusto!"

This all meant nothing to Pandora but it obviously pleased Kitty King.

" 'Gusto' is the right word!" she said. "You should see me striding the stage in me breeches and boots. It brings the audience to their feet, doesn't it, Norvin?"

"They certainly enjoy the sight of you," the Earl replied.

"And there's quite a lot to see!"

"You should be slimming for your next part."

"Not with all the drink you've got in this place," Kitty King answered, "and I could do with one right now."

"Forgive me for appearing inhospitable," the Earl said, "but my cousin has given me a great deal to think about."

"Well, keep that in your mind and not your hands!" Kitty admonished.

The Earl again reached for the bell-pull.

"Champagne!" he said as the door opened.

"I was just bringing it in, M'Lord," the Butler replied.

From behind her two footmen appeared, carrying a large silver ice-bucket in which there were two bottles.

"Well, I don't understand what's going on," Kitty said, throwing herself down on the sofa and crossing her legs so that she displayed a great deal of ankle, "but I've never been one to refuse a friend in need."

"Then you are exactly what my cousin is asking for at this moment," the Earl said.

Kitty King looked at Pandora in a more kindly manner.

"What's wrong with this Parson chap?" she asked. "It seems to me you're well fitted to be his wife."

"That is not true," Pandora said, "and quite frankly I would rather die than marry him!"

"I don't believe it!" Kitty King laughed. "There was never a man yet who was worth *dying* for! You have to try living with them—that's much harder!"

She laughed again, then reached out her hand for the glass of champagne which one of the footmen brought her on a silver salver.

She took it and, lifting it towards the Earl, said:

"Here's to a short life, but a gay one! That's my motto!"

The footman offered Pandora a glass.

She hesitated for a moment.

"Have a little champagne," the Earl said. "I am

sure you need it. It must have taken a great deal of courage to come here."

"I am very grateful to you," Pandora said in a low voice.

"There is no need to be," he answered, "and I have a feeling that you will very likely regret this impulsive act. But why the hell should I care? It is nothing to me what you do—nothing!"

He spoke almost violently and Pandora looked at him in surprise.

Then she told herself that however he behaved, or anyone else in the house for that matter, she would not criticise.

She had turned to the Earl in desperation to throw her a lifeline, and she would always be eternally grateful to him for doing so.

Chapter Two

The house-party arrived a little later, when the Earl and Kitty were still drinking champagne.

There were three young aristocrats, all with titles, but as they were always addressed by their Christian names—Freddie, Clive, and Richard—Pandora found it difficult to sort them out.

They had driven down from London each in his own Phaeton, accompanied by three women as ravishing and attractive in their own way as Kitty was.

Pandora never heard their surnames but it seemed not to matter, as they were usually addressed as "duckie" or "poppet" by their obviously adoring swains.

The three gentlemen declared that their throats were dry from the dust and they were quite exhausted by the drive.

More champagne was hurriedly brought in and they toasted the Earl and Kitty with pointed innuendos and in a manner which Pandora felt was a little embarrassing.

They were, however, all so jolly and so obviously delighted at being at Chart Hall that she found them and their elegant appearance most entertaining.

Then the door opened and another gentleman appeared. Unlike the others, he was announced by the Butler.

"Sir Gilbert Longridge, M'Lord!"

Good-looking and even more smartly arrayed, Sir Gilbert was older than the others.

Yet, watching him cross the room towards the Earl, Pandora thought there was something about him she disliked.

She could not quite understand her feelings, but her father had always said she was very perceptive where people and horses were concerned and that he had seldom known her to make a mistake.

"Alone, Gilbert?" the Earl exclaimed in surprise.

"Fanny cried off," Sir Gilbert replied in a disagreeable voice. "Never again shall I waste my time and my money on a woman who cannot keep her appointments. The Duke can have her, for all I care!"

"He will be delighted," Freddie said. "Though personally, Gilbert, I would think twice about taking on your cast-offs. You indulge them so outrageously that you price them out of the market."

"What is money for, dear boy, except to be spent in enjoyment?" Sir Gilbert asked lazily.

He looked round the room and his eyes fell on Pandora.

For a moment he regarded her without speaking. Then he said:

"Do I perceive that we are now even numbers? How could you be so clairvoyant, my dear Norvin, as to realise I would arrive empty-handed?"

"This is my cousin, Pandora Stratton," the Earl said. "I was not expecting her to be one of the party, but she appeared unexpectedly."

"What could be more delightful than the unexpected?" Sir Gilbert asked suavely.

He walked up to Pandora and taking her hand in his he said:

"You and I were obviously fated for each other, pretty lady, and I have never yet dared to quarrel with fate."

As he touched her Pandora realised that she actively disliked him, and she was wondering how she could extricate her hand from his when the Earl said:

"I do not wish to hurry you, but dinner is at half after seven, and as I have brought Alphonse down with me I would not wish to put him in a rage if the meal is spoilt. You know how temperamental these Frenchmen are."

"I am certainly glad to know that Alphonse is here," Clive remarked. "He is more essential to my comfort even than you, my poppet."

He dropped a kiss as he spoke on the cheek of the woman standing next to him, who with dark curls and flashing eyes was, Pandora thought, almost the most alluring of the new arrivals.

At the same time, she realised that the artifice employed by the three young women, who she guessed from their conversation were also actresses, could be very deceptive.

After watching them for a little while she began to think that they doubtless needed the glamour of the footlights to hide the lines under their eyes and the toughness of their skins, which had not been apparent at first glance.

But in their bonnets festooned with ostrich-feathers, their taffeta cloaks, and their gowns bedecked with lace and ribbons, they were as colourful and eye-catching as a collection of humming-birds.

"We'll go and dress," the one who was called Hettie exclaimed, "and we've brought our best gowns with us to do justice to the ancestral mansion."

She spoke mockingly and the Earl replied:

"You will certainly liven up this mausoleum, which, God knows, is what it needs!"

Pandora looked at him in surprise.

She loved the great house so much and admired its noble proportions and collection of treasures so whole-heartedly that she could hardly believe anyone would disparage such a possession.

As if the Earl sensed what she was feeling, he glanced at her, then said:

"If you are beginning to change your mind and

wish to return home, there is time before you become contaminated."

No-one else heard what he said, and Pandora looking up at him wondered if he realised that she was both bewildered and a little shocked.

Then she said quickly:

"No ... of course not. You are very ... kind to ... have me, and I am sure it will have the ... desired effect on Mr. Witheridge."

"And that, of course, is all that matters," the Earl said.

Pandora quickly hurried after the other women, who were already leaving the room.

Only as she joined them did she look back and see that while the Earl had turned to talk to one of his friends, Sir Gilbert was watching her in a manner that made her nervous.

As they all went up the Great Staircase, which had been used by so many famous Chart ancestors, Pandora gathered from the conversation that only Kitty had been in the house before.

"Lord, but it's big enough to house an Army!" one of the actresses exclaimed.

"Why didn't you ask the whole cast while you were about it, Kitty?" another suggested.

"Sir Edward Trentham has a house which is not far away," Kitty answered. "Gabrielle is staying with him and a whole host of others. They are coming over to dinner."

The others gave a shriek of delight and Pandora understood that Sir Edward was a special favourite.

"Have you heard what he gave Gabrielle last week?" someone asked as they reached the top of the stairs.

"Not another diamond necklace?" someone else replied.

"No—a house in Chelsea, and he's made the deeds over to her too!"

"God, she's lucky!" Hettie exclaimed. "I won't get anything like that out of Richard."

"You should stop him from gambling," Kitty said, "he's far too fond of the cards. It always infuriates me when men lose at the tables what they might have spent on me."

"I agree with you," Hettie replied.

She had hair that was so golden it was almost blinding and her eye-lashes were mascaraed until they stuck out round her blue eyes like little match-sticks.

As they reached the landing Pandora saw that waiting for them was a Housekeeper whom she had never seen before.

She was surprised at not seeing dear old Mrs. Meadowfield, who had been at Chart Hall ever since Pandora could remember.

The new Housekeeper was younger and had the same supercilious, rather insolent manner that Pandora had noticed in the new Butler.

"Good-evening, ladies!" the Housekeeper said, and somehow she made the last word sound like a question. "Let me show you to your rooms."

As the others waited, Kitty said:

"You'll be all right with Mrs. Jenkins. And don't be late! It annoys His Lordship if the soufflés are flat —and that's more than any of us'll be this evening!"

She turned away as she spoke and walked down the corridor to a room that Pandora realised was next to the Master Bed-Room, where her grandfather had always slept.

Mrs. Jenkins showed the other ladies to bed-rooms which, Pandora saw, were each one away from the next, with another room in between.

She wondered at this arrangement, remembering that when her mother had acted as hostess at Chart Hall after her grandmother's death, she had always accommodated the single men and women in separate wings.

She was the last to receive the Housekeeper's attention.

"Now for you, Miss Stratton," she said in a somewhat familiar tone, "I've put you in the Rose Room."

"Oh, I am glad!" Pandora cried. "It was always one of my favourite rooms and I love the view over the garden!"

Mrs. Jenkins looked at her and said:

"Is it really true you're His Lordship's cousin?"

"Yes, indeed," Pandora answered. "My mother was Lady Eveline Chart before she married, and the old Earl was my grandfather."

"You'll find things a bit different now," Mrs. Jenkins said.

Pandora did not know how to answer this. Instead, she went eagerly into the Rose Room to find that her trunk was being unpacked by a maid whom she recognised.

"Good-evening, Mary!" she said. "How nice to find you here! I did not know you were working at the Hall."

"She's new," Mrs. Jenkins said before Mary could speak. "I hope, Miss, if she's not up in her duties you'll tell me, and I'll find someone else."

"I am sure Mary will look after me admirably," Pandora replied.

"These country girls seem very ignorant to me," Mrs. Jenkins said with a sniff.

Mary did not speak until the Housekeeper had left the room. Then she said to Pandora:

"I'm ever so glad to see you, Miss Pandora, that I am! Things be very different here now t' what they was when I used t' come t' give Mother a hand when His Lordship entertained."

"Have you been engaged permanently?" Pandora enquired.

"I hopes so, Miss," Mary replied, "but there's been so many o' the old staff sacked and new ones brought in. None of us in the village seem to know where we are."

"What is your mother doing?" Pandora asked.

"She be helping in the kitchen, Miss. She says as how the Chef gets into such tempers that she be real terrified of him."

"I hear he is French, so tell your mother not to

worry," Pandora said with a smile. "I expect you are both glad of the money."

"We are indeed, Miss!"

Pandora thought that Mary might get into trouble if she stood talking for too long when she had another lady to attend to.

"Come back a little later to do up my gown," she said. "I can manage, as you well know."

"When they told me as you was here, Miss, you could've knocked me down with a feather!" Mary said. "I never thinks I'll see you at Chart Hall, not after the things we've heard of the goings-on and such-like."

Pandora felt it would be extremely disloyal to the Earl if she encouraged Mary to gossip, but she was well aware that the girl was longing to unburden herself.

"Leave me now, Mary, and come back in about a quarter of an hour."

"Very good, Miss."

Mary moved the trunk from the centre of the room and set it against the wall.

"I'll finish the unpacking later, when you've gone down to dinner, Miss," she said.

As she reached the door she added:

"I'm glad you're here, Miss, real glad!"

She left and Pandora with a little frown between her brows went on undressing.

There had been a note of fear in Mary's voice that she had not liked. It made her feel worried and apprehensive as to what was happening at Chart Hall.

She knew she did not like the new servants and it was not just prejudice because the old staff had been dismissed.

She wondered what her father and mother would have thought of the Earl.

He was certainly very strange—perhaps "eccentric" was the right word—and yet, Pandora told herself, she did not dislike him as she had disliked on sight Sir Gilbert Longridge.

'It is no use my having fads and fancies about

these people,' she thought. 'I came here because I was desperate, and I must make the best of them, whatever they are like.'

She could not, however, help feeling that it was all very strange, but she was certain of one thing—Prosper Witheridge would disapprove whole-heartedly of Kitty, Hettie, Lottie, and Caro, as the third actress was called.

She had heard him say that Play-Houses were a snare for the unwary and a meeting-place of sinners.

"I am sure after this he will not wish to own me," she declared.

Her thoughts shied away from what her uncle and aunt would say when they knew where she had been.

"If the Earl will keep me," she declared, "I will stay until Friday morning, for if I go back to the Palace earlier, Prosper will be waiting to berate me."

She could imagine how sanctimonious and pompous he would be about it. Almost as if thinking about him conjured him up, when Mary returned a little while later she said:

"I was to tell you, Miss, as there's a gentleman waiting to see you downstairs."

"A gentleman?" Pandora asked in surprise.

"The footman says he's a Parson, Miss."

Pandora's heart gave a frightened leap.

There was no doubt who her visitor was, but she had not expected him to be here so quickly.

Then she realised it was seven o'clock and if he had arrived back at Lindchester a little earlier than she had expected he would have had time to get here after reading her letter.

"I should have had it delivered tomorrow," she told herself, but now it was too late.

Mary was fastening her evening-gown.

It had been one of her mother's that she had altered for herself and she had packed it because she considered it to be her best. She felt too it was somehow right that it should be worn once again at Chart Hall.

She was however well aware that it would seem very simple and perhaps out-of-date beside the flamboyant gowns that the actresses would wear, but their appearance, while colourful, was undoubtedly vulgar, and she knew that neither her father nor her mother would have approved of them.

She was too agitated at the thought of Prosper Witheridge waiting for her downstairs to look at her reflection in the mirror.

Instead, she clasped round her long neck the little band of turquoise-blue velvet which matched the ribbons of her gown, then she said to Mary:

"I must go down. Is there anyone else downstairs?"

"It's unlikely, Miss. The housemaids say the ladies are never ready till the last moment, 'cause they takes such hours apainting their faces."

Pandora stood irresolute for a moment, then she said:

"Do you think, Mary, you could get one of the footmen to tell His Lordship who is here?"

"Yes, of course, Miss, and he'll tell His Lordship's valet."

"Say that the gentleman to whom I sent a letter has called here to see me."

"Very good, Miss," Mary answered.

Pandora hesitated.

She wanted not to go downstairs until perhaps the Earl volunteered to go with her.

Then she told herself she must not be a coward, and it was impossible to expect a man she had just met, even though he was her cousin, to involve himself in her personal problems.

Holding her head high, but at the same time aware that her heart was thumping uncomfortably in her breast, she walked slowly down the Great Staircase.

Somehow the sight of her ancestors looking down at her from their portraits on the walls seemed to give her courage.

'Help me!' Pandora cried to them silently. 'Why should I be afraid of a man like Prosper Witheridge?'

But she was afraid, and her fingers were cold as she reached the hall. The Butler who was waiting there said to her:

"I've put your caller, Miss, in the Small Salon."

He spoke in a way which told Pandora he was enjoying what he felt was a drama, and she replied with a cold dignity:

"Thank you. I presume that we are meeting in the Silver Salon before dinner?"

"That's right, Miss," the Butler replied.

She thought that he looked at her in a slightly more respectful manner, realising she was used to the ways of the house.

He opened the door of the Small Salon, which was a room her mother had loved and where she had often received visitors when her grandfather had been too ill to entertain them himself.

Prosper Witheridge was standing with his back to the marble mantelpiece, looking, Pandora realised with a sinking of her heart, particularly aggressive.

He was so angry that there was a frown between his protruding eyes, which were set too close together, and there was a hard line to his thin lips.

Pandora heard the door shut behind her and she forced herself to walk slowly and in a dignified manner towards him.

He waited until she had reached him. Then he said in a voice in which his anger was barely concealed:

"Have you gone raving mad? Are you crazy that you should have come here?"

"As I told you in my letter, I am staying with my cousin."

"Then pack your box. I will take you back immediately," Prosper Witheridge said sharply.

"My cousin has asked me to stay here as his guest, which I intend to do."

"I can only assume you have taken leave of your senses," he replied. "You know full well it is something which your aunt and uncle would not countenance,

and your sensibility should tell you this is not a house
in which you should stay."

"It is the house which belonged to my grandfather."

"But his place has been taken by a dissolute Rake
and I will not allow you to remain in his company
for one more second."

"You have no authority to stop me."

"As your future husband ..." Prosper Witheridge
began.

"I will not marry you! Let me make it quite clear
here and now," Pandora interrupted, "that I would
not marry you if you were the last man in the world!"

For a moment the Honourable Prosper Witheridge
was stunned into silence.

He was a very conceited man and so many wom-
en had flattered and fawned on him that it had never
for one moment crossed his mind that Pandora would
not fall into his arms gladly and gratefully.

"Do you know what you are saying?" he asked.

The surprise in his voice would have amused Pandora if she had not found it difficult to think of anything but her thumping heart.

"I will not ... marry you!" she said, a determined
note in her voice.

"After you have stayed here it is unlikely that
any man will offer you marriage."

"I understood that when I came."

"You are too young and innocent to know what
you are saying or what you are doing," Prosper
Witheridge said, almost as if he were explaining her
actions to himself.

"I do understand, and I have come here deliberately, because I wished to come and because whatever my uncle and aunt may say ... I will not ...
marry ... you!"

"You are talking arrant nonsense!" Prosper Witheridge snapped, and now he began to lose his temper.
"I am taking you back with me now, and on return
to the Palace I shall lock you in your bed-room, where
you will stay until your uncle returns."

"I will not allow you to do anything of the sort!" Pandora answered defiantly.

"You have no choice," Prosper Witheridge said, and there was a grim note in his voice that she did not miss.

As he spoke he reached out and caught hold of her arm.

His action took her by surprise. She had never imagined he would actually touch her or, as she now realised, drag her away with him.

She struggled and his fingers bit into the softness of her skin.

"How dare you touch me!" she cried. "Let me go!"

"You will come with me!" Prosper Witheridge said. "And I only hope that when your uncle returns he will punish you as you so richly deserve for your disgraceful behaviour!"

As he spoke, he started to drag her across the Salon, Pandora fighting every inch of the way.

She was very small and he was large, and she realised despairingly that it was a losing battle.

"Let me go!" she cried, and screamed as he pulled her roughly to the door.

Even as they reached it, it opened and the Earl stood there.

He was in evening-dress and he looked not only tidier than he had previously, but almost resplendent in a meticulously tied white cravat and a closely fitting evening-coat over the long, hose-like pantaloons which had just come into fashion.

He stood still in the doorway, and Prosper Witheridge, dragging Pandora by the arm, was forced also to come to a standstill.

"May I enquire what is going on here?" the Earl asked, his voice icy.

"You are the Earl of Chartwood?" Prosper Witheridge asked without releasing Pandora.

"It is for me to ask the questions," the Earl replied, "as you have come here uninvited."

"I have come," Prosper Witheridge replied, "to

take a young girl, who has no right to impose upon Your Lordship, back to where she belongs."

"On whose authority?"

"On mine!" he replied. "I am the private Chaplain to the Very Reverend Bishop of Lindchester!"

"How nice for you!" the Earl said mockingly. "And does that position entitle you to go round abducting young women from the homes of their relatives?"

"I am not abducting Miss Stratton," Prosper Witheridge answered. "Her uncle, the Bishop, left her in my charge and I have just returned to Lindchester to find that she has embarked on this most regrettable escapade, which will deeply grieve those who out of the kindness of their hearts offered her a decent home."

"Are you insinuating that my house is an indecent one?" the Earl asked.

There was a steely note in his voice, but Pandora knew by the look in his eyes that he was enjoying himself.

Prosper Witheridge was too angry to be cautious.

"Your Lordship is well aware," he replied, "that Chart Hall is not a proper place for a young and innocent girl."

"Is that your personal opinion?" the Earl questioned. "Because if it is, I should be interested to hear on what grounds you base such an assumption."

Prosper Witheridge looked uncomfortable.

"There is no point in bandying words, Your Lordship," he said. "I will, with your permission, take Miss Stratton home. I will arrange for her belongings to be collected tomorrow morning."

"I do not give my permission!" the Earl replied. "My cousin is here as my guest, and here she may stay for as long as it suits her!"

"You cannot mean that!" Prosper Witheridge ejaculated.

"I should have thought that as an educated man you could understand plain English," the Earl replied.

For the first time since they had been speaking, Prosper Witheridge released Pandora's arm.

"This conversation is absurd," he said harshly. "What Your Lordship does in your own private life is your affair, but Miss Stratton is too young and too unsophisticated to understand."

"To understand what?" the Earl asked.

"That Your Lordship's life-style and the friends with whom you associate are alien to anything she has ever known or imagined."

"What do you know about my life-style and my friends?" the Earl asked.

He spoke mildly, almost pleasantly.

"I know," Prosper Witheridge replied, raising his voice, "that it stinks in the nostrils of those who are godly! That what takes place here in this ancestral house is under the aegis of Satan himself."

He roared the last words, and as he finished the Earl threw back his head and laughed.

"Very effective!" he said. "How much the spinsters of Lindchester must enjoy the fire and brimstone of Hell that you envisage for such sinners as myself! Well, Mr. Parson, let me make it quite clear: I am not impressed by your blusterings, and as I am just about to take my cousin into dinner, I suggest you return to those who appreciate your eloquence."

The Earl spoke scathingly, but he did not raise his voice.

"If I leave I am taking Miss Stratton with me," Prosper Witheridge roared.

The Earl was just about to reply when there was the patter of feet across the hall and Kitty and Caro appeared behind the Earl in the doorway.

"I thought we were to meet in the Sal—" Kitty began, then saw Prosper Witheridge and exclaimed: "Oh, who is this?"

"This gentleman," the Earl replied, "is a messenger from the Lord to tell us that we will burn in the fires of Hell, and he is not prepared to offer us so much as a drop of cold water."

"Cold water?" Caro cried. "Who wants that? I am dying—just dying—for a glass of champagne!"

She linked her arm through the Earl's as if she intended to drag him away to find it for her.

Pandora glanced at Prosper Witheridge's face and almost laughed aloud. There was no doubt that he was shocked at Kitty and Caro's appearance, and it was in fact not surprising.

Pandora had never seen women wearing gowns which were cut so low and were so revealing.

There seemed to be a boundless expanse of white chest ornamented with jewelled necklaces, and the curves of their breasts could be seen clearly as the ribbons of their high-waisted gowns began only half-way down the valley between them.

Their faces were painted with what seemed almost white masks and their eye-lashes were mascaraed in a way which made their eyes look enormous, especially as they were outlined in black as if they were on the stage.

Their hair was dressed with jewels and the glittering bracelets on their wrists only seemed to accentuate the nakedness of their arms.

Pandora thought that even to her father's eyes they would have seemed fantastic, but to Prosper Witheridge they were representative of everything he denounced so fervently about the Play-Houses and the temptations in the way of those who attended them.

"Our guests will be arriving at any moment," Kitty said. "Are you going to ask him to join us—he'll give us a laugh, if nothing else!"

She jerked her thumb at Prosper Witheridge as she spoke, and the Earl replied:

"What a good idea! Do stay for dinner, Witheridge, and beguile us with your intimate knowledge of Satan's ways. I am sure that even such ardent adherents of the Devil as ourselves will learn something new."

Prosper Witheridge drew himself up.

He had gone pale with anger and disgust as he

realised that to answer would merely make him a laughing-stock.

"I have nothing more to say, My Lord," he said. "I will leave this house and this unfortunate girl, who has no idea of the depths of the cesspool in which she is preparing to drown herself."

He took a step forward as he spoke, and the Earl made way for him.

"Do not let us keep you, Mr. Witheridge," he said.

Prosper Witheridge turned to Pandora.

"You will regret this day!" he thundered. "You will remember for the rest of your life that the choice was yours to go upwards to the God who made you, or downwards to the Devil who has tempted you!"

His voice seemed to vibrate round the room. Then, as if he fancied himself a crusader defeated for the moment by the hordes of evil, he strode away.

He crossed the hall, snatching his black hat from the footman who held it out to him before he passed through the front door and down the steps to where a carriage was waiting.

"Hell's bells!" Kitty exclaimed. "If you don't want a drink after that—I do!"

"He was creepy!" Caro exclaimed. "I feel as if he cursed me!"

"He has cursed us all," the Earl replied, "and most especially Pandora."

He looked at her questioningly as he spoke, but Pandora gave a little sigh of sheer relief.

"He certainly will not want to marry me now."

"He is more likely to have you branded as a scarlet woman and flogged through the streets of Lindchester," the Earl replied.

"Did they really do things like that in the 'bad old days'?" Kitty asked.

"It happens today," the Earl replied, "so look out!"

"You're trying to frighten me," Kitty protested, "besides, except for my breeches and you, I'm almost respectable."

" 'Almost' being the operative word," the Earl said. "But Caro is right, we all need a drink. These dramatics before dinner are extremely fatiguing."

He walked towards the Salon and Pandora followed him.

She felt a little shaken by what had occurred, and the fury and contempt in Prosper Witheridge's voice had affected her, even though she told herself the only thing that really mattered was that she was free of him.

There was now the worry of what her uncle and aunt would say, but she knew there was now no chance of Prosper forgiving her or, as he had intended, with the Bishop's permission paying his addresses to her.

He was extremely ambitious and there was no doubt that one day he might end up a Bishop, but not if he had a wife whose behaviour was scandalous, and that was how it would appear in the eyes of those who lived in Lindchester.

'I do not care!' Pandora thought bravely.

They had no sooner reached the Salon where the rest of the house-party had already gathered than Sir Edward Trentham arrived with his house-party.

Pandora remembered when she saw him that he had acquired an Estate in the County just before she had left Chart.

The previous owner had been a friend of her father's, and now she remembered hearing that he had lost all his money at the gaming-tables. She thought Sir Edward must have been the winner.

It was easy to guess by the effusive manner in which the actresses greeted him that he was not only rich but generous. They all kissed him, throwing their arms round his neck.

Pandora saw that he was a man of about forty, somewhat flamboyantly dressed, as if he wished to appear younger than his age.

"Delighted to see you in your rightful background, Norvin," he said to the Earl. "I have never been here before. Damned impressive house! What are you going to do with it?"

"Put up with it, I suppose!" the Earl replied.

There was a shriek of laughter at this.

"That cannot be much of a hardship," Sir Edward said. "I would not mind taking it from you in a game of chance."

"Unfortunately, it is entailed," the Earl replied, "but I assure you, my successor will get little more than the bare walls."

Pandora felt she could not have heard him aright. What did he mean? Why did he speak in such a manner of this wonderful house which in itself was a page of history?

She wanted to ask for an explanation, but at that moment Sir Gilbert was beside her.

"I intend to look after you this evening, little Pandora," he said, "and I cannot tell you how much the thought delights me."

He took her hand as he spoke and raised it to his lips. Pandora felt a shudder go through her when his mouth touched her skin.

She felt the same way, she thought, about Prosper Witheridge, and wondered why she had the misfortune to attract such horrible men.

"I expected to find myself lonely and unwanted tonight," Sir Gilbert was saying, "but instead I know that I shall be entranced and delighted in a manner which makes me excited even to think of it."

His face was very near to hers and Pandora took a step backwards.

She hoped he would not be sitting next to her at dinner, but she found to her dismay that he was on her left, although she was relieved to find that the Earl was on her right.

Kitty was on their host's other side and monopolised him by making him laugh and whispering in his ear in a manner which Pandora knew would never have happened at her mother's dining-table.

So she was forced, whether she liked it or not, to talk to Sir Gilbert, and he made the most of it.

"You are very lovely!" he said. "Your eyes are a complete contrast to your hair, and they really are purple in the candlelight."

He paused before he asked in an insinuating manner:

"Can I make them glow with the fires of desire?"

"That sounds like an extract from the sort of novel you would not find in this Library," Pandora said coldly.

"Are you being provocative or merely unkind?" Sir Gilbert enquired.

"I think really such questions make me feel uncomfortable," Pandora answered.

She told herself she was not afraid of him, that she just found him a bore. She would much rather look round and think how wonderful it was to be back in the huge Dining-Room where her grandfather and grandmother used to entertain when she was a little girl.

There had not been many parties after her Uncle George was killed at Waterloo.

After her grandmother died, her grandfather had sat alone at the end of the long table where the Earl was sitting now and old Burrows had laid out the family silver.

He would polish it with his rheumatic hands, but it reflected not guests but only the coats-of-arms embroidered on the empty chairs.

"How many men have made love to you?" Sir Gilbert was murmuring against Pandora's ear.

"No-one has made love to me!" Pandora replied firmly. "And I would much rather talk about horses. Do you keep many, Sir Gilbert?"

He laughed as if he was amused by her attempt to evade him.

"At the moment I am only interested in one particularly attractive little filly," he answered, "who has not yet been broken to the bridle. May I say that is something I shall greatly enjoy doing?"

"I do not understand what you are saying," Pandora replied.

She was glad when Sir Gilbert's conversation was interrupted by the footmen offering dishes that she realised were not only delicious but different from anything she had eaten before.

Her mother had taught her to cook and Pandora tried to guess the ingredients that had gone into the sauce with the tenderloin of veal.

She wondered if it would be possible to meet the Chef before she left Chart Hall and ask him for some of his recipes.

There was no hope of improving the dull, stodgy fare that her aunt ordered at the Palace, but perhaps one day she would be able to cook for someone who thought good food was an art, as her father had done.

"I was telling you," Sir Gilbert said in a purring tone which she told herself she disliked, "how much I long to kiss you and to teach you, my wild, un-broken filly, about love."

He really was becoming rather tiresome, Pandora thought, and besides, he had had too much to drink.

In fact, as the meal came to an end, looking round the Dining-Room she was quite certain that the majority of the gentlemen were what her father would have called "foxed."

They were all rather red in the face and had a "swimmy" look in their eyes, which reminded her uncomfortably of the manner in which Prosper Witheridge looked at her.

Their high carvats were creased and some of them had undone their waist-coats, which she thought was a shocking breach of good manners.

The women too seemed to have got noisier, and their voices were more shrill.

By the time the dessert was being taken round— the huge peaches which she remembered as a child, and great bunches of muscat grapes—the décolletages of the actresses seemed even lower than when they had shocked Prosper Witheridge.

When they bent forward to shout across the table, Pandora blushed to see what they revealed, and she was thankful that her own gown with its short sleeves was cut discreetly and her appearance was unlikely to offend anyone.

At the same time, she thought she must look very plain and unattractive in contrast.

'A country sparrow,' she thought to herself with a smile, 'mixed up with exotic birds-of-Paradise.'

She must have smiled at her own thoughts, because the Earl, turning to her for almost the first time since they had sat down to dinner, asked:

"What is amusing you?"

"I was not really amused," Pandora answered, "I was just thinking that I was a little out-of-place amongst such colourful ladies."

"It was your own choice."

He spoke harshly.

"I am not complaining," Pandora said quickly. "You must not think that, when you have been so kind. It is just that this is so very different from the dinner-parties at the Palace."

"I should hope so!" the Earl remarked.

"We used to have lovely parties at the Vicarage when we lived there," Pandora said. "Papa knew how to make people laugh, and Mama loved entertaining when we could afford it."

"Were you very poor?" the Earl questioned.

"We had to save every penny so that Papa and Mama could have horses," Pandora answered.

She was remembering that it was those same horses that had taken her father and mother from her, and for a moment a shadow darkened her eyes.

She found that the Earl was watching her.

"Have I many more relations like you?" he enquired.

"Most of them are old and rather stuffy," Pandora admitted, "and I have not seen any of the more interesting ones since Grandpapa gave up entertaining."

"When was that?"

"After Waterloo, when Uncle George was killed."

"A very fortunate occurrence, as far as I was concerned."

"I cannot imagine anything more fortunate or lucky for anyone than to inherit this house," Pandora said quietly, "and to realise you are the head of a family that has existed for so many generations."

"And of course you expect me to make a commendable head and embellish the family name," the Earl said, and now there was no doubt that he was jeering at her.

"Why should you want to do anything else," Pandora asked, "especially when you have been so lucky?"

He stared at her in what she thought was surprise, and at that moment there was a shriek from Hettie at the other end of the table.

The gentleman sitting on her left had inadvertently, or drunkenly, upset a glass of wine into her lap.

"You stupid bastard!" she exclaimed furiously, and picking up the china dessert-plate which was in front of her she broke it over his head.

There was a roar of laughter from everyone round the table and cries of:

"Serves him right!" "Teach him to behave better, Hettie."

Pandora drew in her breath.

"That was the pink Sèvres!" she said almost to herself. "Mama always warned the servants to be especially careful with it."

She spoke in a very low voice, but the Earl heard her.

He bent towards her.

"Go to bed, Pandora," he said. "Do not say good-night, just leave the room without making a fuss."

She looked at him, wide-eyed, and was prepared to protest that she wanted to stay, but there was an air of authority about him that she had not noticed before.

"Good-night, Cousin Norvin," she said quietly, "and thank you for being so very kind to me."

Chapter Three

"I'm not . . . tired! I don't . . . want to . . . go to . . . bed!"

Kitty clung to the newel at the turn of the bannister as she spoke, but the Earl disengaged her fingers and half-carried, half-pulled her up the stairs.

Like the rest of the party, Kitty was very drunk.

They had seen off Sir Edward and his friends with shrieks, cries, and hiccups which had echoed round the marble hall and made even the flags from the ancient battlements seem to sway with the noise.

Now the house-party were climbing up the Great Staircase and the tired servants were locking and bolting the front door, preferring to scurry off to their own quarters.

The gentlemen had more command over their actions than the women had.

Caro had collapsed altogether and Richard was carrying her rather unsteadily.

Hettie was still at the noisy stage, protesting, like Kitty, that she had no wish to go to bed and that she wanted another drink.

The Earl had got Kitty to the landing when she struggled unexpectedly against him, and, as he had not a firm hold on her, she collapsed against a valuable piece of furniture, knocking over a vase of flowers.

"I want to . . . dance," she said. "Let's go and . . . dance."

"You had better go to bed, Kitty," the Earl said.

"I won't! I won't!" she cried defiantly.

Then she swayed against him so that he was forced to support her with both arms.

"I'll give you a hand, M'Lord," a voice said, and Mrs. Jenkins put her arm round Kitty's waist.

Together they propelled her down the corridor and into the magnificent room which had always been occupied by the Countesses of Chartwood.

As they reached the bed, the Earl realised that Kitty was no longer fighting. Her eyes were shut and she had gone limp.

"Out cold!" Mrs. Jenkins remarked. "I'll put her to bed, Your Lordship."

She too spoke in a slurred way, which made the Earl look at her sharply.

The Housekeeper's face was very red and her hair was untidy. There was no doubt that she had been drinking.

She picked up Kitty's legs by the ankles and flung them down with almost a disdainful action.

"You won't be hearing from her, M'Lord, 'til morning," she said in an impertinent manner, "so Your Lordship'll be sleeping—alone."

The Earl frowned but he did not answer, and after a moment Mrs. Jenkins added:

"Everyone else is tied up nice and tidy. One gentleman, Sir Gilbert Something-or-other, gives me a guinea to tell him in which room your cousin is sleeping."

The Earl stiffened.

He seemed about to say something. Then, as if he thought any rebuke would be useless, seeing the state Mrs. Jenkins was in, he turned and went from the room.

He walked down the corridor to where he knew the Rose Room was situated.

He had arranged the other bed-rooms himself, but he would not have known where Pandora was had not she said at dinner:

"It is so lovely to be back here and to sleep in the Rose Room, where I have slept before."

"Did you often stay here when you had a house in the village?" he had asked.

"Only when Papa and Mama went away on what they called 'a second honeymoon.' They so loved being alone together, but they could not afford to do so very often."

The Earl had been about to ask her more about her life, but Kitty had demanded his attention, jealous that he should speak to any woman other than herself.

Now he reached the Rose Room, which was at the end of the corridor where the central part of the great house joined the West Wing.

For a moment he hesitated outside the door.

There was no sound, but there was a light beneath the door and he was surprised that Pandora was still awake.

Very gently he tried the handle; it turned, and he opened the door and went in.

There were only two candles, both of which were guttering low on the table beside the bed.

Then as he looked round the silk curtains which fell from a corola fixed to the ceiling, he saw that Pandora was asleep.

She was lying against the pillows with her fair hair falling over her shoulders, and by her hand on top of the sheet was an open book.

The Earl drew a little nearer.

He stood looking down at her small heart-shaped face and at her long, natural eye-lashes like half-moons silhouetted against her pale, translucent skin.

The candlelight seemed to pick out the gold in her hair, but it was very unlike the brilliance of Hettie's and was instead the colour of dawn when it first appears in the East.

As if his scrutiny reached through her dreams and awakened her, Pandora opened her eyes.

For a moment she looked at him drowsily as if she was not certain who he was, then she gave a little exclamation and sat up.

"I fell asleep without blowing out ... the candles," she said in a horrified voice. "It is something Mama was always insistent I should not do in case I set the house on fire. Oh, I am ... sorry!"

Her voice was so self-accusing that the Earl smiled.

"You were tired," he said. "There is nothing more exhausting than being worried and perhaps afraid."

"I am ashamed that I should have been afraid of Prosper Witheridge."

She was quite unselfconscious, the Earl thought, of the fact that he was in her bed-room, and, for although he was her cousin, he was still a man.

She was wearing a lawn nightgown which fastened at the neck and had a little collar edged with lace and long sleeves with lace-edged frills that fell over her wrists.

She looked very young and very innocent, and after a moment the Earl said:

"I saw a light under your door and thought you must be still awake."

Pandora looked down at her book.

"I took a book from the Library when I came upstairs. I was longing to read it again. It is one of my favourites."

"What is it called?" the Earl enquired.

"*Paradise Regained*. Do you not think Milton describes very convincingly what he imagined?"

"It is a long time since I read Milton," the Earl answered cautiously. "I think I remember *Paradise Lost* better."

"I hate that book! It is so depressing, so frightening, in fact it is rather like listening to Prosper Witheridge!"

"It is unlikely that you will have to listen to him again."

"He will denounce me to my uncle in an even more violent fashion than he spoke about me ... downstairs."

"Forget him for tonight, at any rate," the Earl

said. "And as you like *Paradise Regained* so much, let me make you a present of it."

He saw the look of delight in Pandora's eyes. Then, when she would have thanked him, she checked the words.

"It is kind of you, but it is a very valuable book and it belongs here in the collection."

"What does that matter?" the Earl enquired. "I am sure you will appreciate it far more than I or my guests would."

There was a sarcastic twist to his lips as he thought of Kitty lying unconscious.

He knew she could hardly write, and it was very doubtful if she could read anything more difficult than the figures on a bank-note.

"If the books are borrowed and not returned, or are given away," Pandora said after a moment, "it would be depriving your son of his inheritance and of course your grandsons and their sons."

"My son?" the Earl repeated in surprise.

"Grandpapa told me a long time ago, when I was a very little girl," Pandora explained, "that the Earls of Chartwood do not really possess what is here in the house. They are only Guardians of all the wonderful treasures for those who come after them."

She looked anxiously at the Earl before she added:

"Perhaps you thought it impertinent of me when I was upset at dinner because the plate was broken, but the service was given to one of our ancestors by Madame de Pompadour, who took a great interest in the Sèvres factory."

She looked at the Earl with a worried look in her eyes in case he should be angry. Then she said:

"Mama always said they were too good to be used except on very . . . very special . . . occasions."

"Tonight was a very special occasion as far as I am concerned," the Earl said.

Pandora had the feeling that he was speaking automatically, just to argue with her.

"You enjoyed yourself?" she asked, and she was not being sarcastic.

"Very much!" he said defiantly.

"What did you . . . do after . . . I left?"

The question was almost wistful, as if she thought she had missed something.

The Earl hesitated and as he did so the door of the room opened and Sir Gilbert Longridge came in.

He had changed from his evening-clothes into a long robe of red brocade with the white frill of his nightshirt showing above it.

He stopped in the doorway at the sight of the Earl, and Pandora turned her head to look at him in astonishment.

The Earl rose from where he had seated himself at the farthest corner of the bed.

"I am afraid you have lost your way, Gilbert," he said genially. "It is very easy to do so in this large house."

"I did not expect to find you here, Norvin," Sir Gilbert replied.

"I was just saying good-night to my cousin. As you know, she went to bed early, but unfortunately she fell asleep and left the candles burning."

Sir Gilbert obviously was not listening to what the Earl was saying. He was only staring at him in a glowering manner.

The Earl walked towards him and as he reached him Sir Gilbert said:

"You have Kitty. I cannot think why I should be left out!"

"I will see what I can do for you tomorrow," the Earl replied, "but now Pandora wishes to go to sleep, and so do I."

There was that authoritative note in his voice which Pandora had noticed before when he sent her to bed.

For a moment Sir Gilbert did not move. Then with what was an oath beneath his breath he turned and walked from the room.

The Earl looked at Pandora. Her eyes were very wide in her small face.

"I am now going to my own room," he said, "and as soon as I have gone, you are to lock the door. Do you understand? Get out of bed and lock the door. And do not open it until you are called in the morning."

For a moment she did not understand. Then he saw the colour come into her face.

"Do you . . . think Sir Gilbert might . . . come back?" she asked almost beneath her breath.

"It is very easy for people to get lost in these long corridors," the Earl replied evasively.

He walked through the door.

"Lock the door, Pandora, and do not open it again until the morning. Is that clear?"

"Yes, Cousin Norvin, and I am . . . sorry I left the . . . candles burning."

"I will forgive you this time. Sleep well, Pandora."

He left, and obediently Pandora pushed back the sheets and crossed the room.

She turned the key in the lock and as she did so she thought with a shiver how frightening it would have been if the Earl had not been there when Sir Gilbert had arrived.

He might have tried to kiss her—in fact she was sure he would have done so after all he had said at dinner—and she knew she would have been afraid, very afraid, and perhaps no-one would have heard her cries.

"It must have been Mama who sent Cousin Norvin to see if I was all right," she told herself. "It would have been terrible if I had set the house on fire and perhaps even more terrible if Sir Gilbert had found me alone."

She got back into bed but now it was difficult to fall asleep again.

She found herself thinking of what had happened during the day, then worrying as to what other damage might have been done after she left the Din-ing-Room.

She wondered if it would be possible to persuade the Butler to put away the Sèvres service and re-place it with the very attractive but not so priceless one that had always been in use in her grandfa-ther's time.

Then she told herself she had no right to do so, and it would be extremely presumptuous of her to interfere in any way with the running of the house-hold.

She had no standing here and she should just be grateful that her cousin had been so kind to her.

She snuggled down against the pillows.

'I am sure he is not as bad as they say he is, or as he pretends to be,' she thought.

She had a feeling that he was putting on an act of being so wicked. But why? What was his motive?

Some words of Milton came to her mind.

> *Wisest men*
> *Have erred, and by bad women been deceived.*

Was that what had happened? she wondered.

She was still puzzling over it when she fell asleep.

*   *   *

Pandora was awakened by a knock on the door and started nervously, only to realise that the sun was golden at the sides of the curtains and it was morn-ing.

She jumped out of bed to unlock the door and found Mary standing there with a breakfast-tray in her hands.

"Breakfast in bed?" Pandora exclaimed. "How exciting! It is something I have not enjoyed for years."

Without waiting for Mary to reply, she hurried across the room and got back into bed, patting up the

pillows behind her back and smoothing the creases
from the sheets.

Mary put down the tray in front of her and
Pandora looked at it with delight.

There was not only a silver dish with a cover,
there was toast in a silver rack, golden butter, honey,
and a huge peach.

It all reminded her of the time when she had
been laid up, before her mother had died, with an
attack of laryngitis.

The Doctor had said she was to stay in bed and
keep warm. Her mother had spoilt her with all sorts
of delicacies, so that she had looked forward to meal-
times almost greedily.

She was just about to reminisce about it with
Mary, when looking at the maid she saw that her
eyes were swollen and red with tears.

"What is the matter, Mary?"

"Nothin' I can tell you, Miss Pandora," Mary answered, "but this be a real wicked place, an' that's
th' truth!"

"What has happened?" Pandora asked.

"I shouldn't be tellin' you such things."

"What things?"

Mary twisted her fingers in her apron and Pandora saw that tears were filling her eyes.

She was evidently thinking over what she
should do, then suddenly she burst into tears.

"It's—cruel and—hard, Miss Pandora—that's what
it is—and wicked! I never knowed such wickedness
existed!"

Pandora moved the breakfast-tray to the other
side of the bed.

"You must tell me what has happened, Mary. You
know I will help you if I can."

"It's that Mrs. Jenkins, Miss. She's a bad woman!
Really bad, she bel"

"What has she done?" Pandora asked.

Mary looked towards the door and saw that she
had left it partly open when she came in with the
tray.

Swiftly she ran to it and shut it, and with the tears running down her cheeks she came back to the bed-side.

"I daren't tell me mother what she says t' me this mornin'," Mary began, her voice heavy with tears.

"But you must tell me," Pandora insisted.

"Well, Miss, I comes here two days ago t' help in th' house, an' as you guessed, we were glad o' th' money. Father's been sacked by His Lordship's new agent."

"Sacked?" Pandora questioned. "But your father has worked in the gardens ever since I can remember."

"Th' new agent, Mr. Anstey he's called, has brought in a lot o' his own friends, Miss, an' given them all cottages on th' Estate."

"What do you mean . . . given them cottages?"

"Turned out th' old people—me Granny being one o' them."

"Mrs. Clay! Do you mean to say that Mrs. Clay has been turned out of her cottage?"

"Yes, Miss, an' there's nowhere else for her t' go except th' Workhouse if me father doesn't get a job soon."

"It is disgraceful!" Pandora exclaimed. "Mrs. Clay and your grandfather worked on the Estate all their lives."

"I know, Miss, but that don't count for nothing nowadays."

"Then it should!" Pandora said positively. "Now, tell me what has upset you, Mary."

"I oughtn't rightly t' speak o' it, not t' a lady like yourself."

"Tell me!"

"Last night, Miss, knowin' what I'd heard of th' goings-on in the household, I locks me door when I goes t' bed."

"That was a sensible thing to do," Pandora said, remembering how Sir Gilbert had come to her room.

" 'Twas very late, an' I'd been asleep a long

time," Mary went on, "when Mrs. Jenkins comes aknocking.

" 'Are you there, Mary?' she says, an' I knows by th' way she's aspeaking she'd had a lot t' drink!

"I didn't answer because I were afraid o' what she would be atelling me t' do."

"What do you mean . . . what she would tell you to do?" Pandora asked, curious.

Mary twisted her apron more nervously than ever, then she said:

"I wasn't exactly sure, Miss, but seein' as what I've heard, it was that right enough."

"I do not understand," Pandora said again.

"This morning, Miss, as soon as Mrs. Jenkins gets down she sends for me an' she tells me that one o' th' gentlemen wanted me last night t' go t' his room.

" 'I'm a good girl, Ma'am,' I says.

"It makes her angry when I speaks like that, an' she tells me either I does as she orders or else I can pack me bags an' leave!"

Mary burst into a fresh flood of weeping before she said almost incoherently:

" 'If you leave,' Mrs. Jenkins says to me, 'then you an' your family can clear out o' that cottage. It's wanted for someone who'll behave as I say, so make that clear!' "

Pandora gasped from sheer astonishment and Mary said piteously:

"What can I do, Miss? If we're all turned out, where can we go?"

Pandora was silent.

At the same time, she felt an anger rising within her that was different from anything she had ever felt before.

Now she understood why the last time she had been to Chart the villagers had seemed fearful and afraid to speak of what was happening. Now she knew why people like Prosper Witheridge denounced what was happening at Chart Hall.

She threw back the bed-clothes and got out of bed.

"Listen to me, Mary," she said. "Say nothing to

Mrs. Jenkins until I have spoken to His Lordship. I cannot believe he knows that this sort of thing is happening."

"He'll not care, Miss. He sacked Mr. Farrow, said he was too old, and gave Mr. Anstey his place."

"What happened to Mr. Farrow?" Pandora asked, taking off her nightgown.

"I thinks he were ready t' retire, Miss, but he always hoped as how his son'd take over."

"Of course ... Michael Farrow!" Pandora exclaimed.

"He be a kind gentleman, Miss. Kind t' everyone who turned t' him in trouble. Not like this Mr. Anstey."

"What else has he done?" Pandora asked sharply.

"He's raised th' rents, Miss, an' if anyone's late in payin' even by a few days, he pushes them out."

She glanced at the door, then back at Pandora, and her voice dropped to a whisper.

"He's got a wife, Miss, but he's sweet on Mrs. Jenkins. That's why what her says goes."

Pandora did not answer. She was moving towards the washing-stand.

"If you're agetting up, Miss," Mary said hurriedly as if she remembered her duties, "I'll fetch you some hot water, unless you wants a bath?"

"I have no time to wait for hot water or a bath," Pandora answered.

She poured the cold water from the china ewer into the basin and washed despite Mary's protests.

"Go on with what you were telling me," she said. "I want to hear everything now."

"Well, Miss, Mother's said for a long time that things be all wrong downstairs. Mr. Anstey sends away Mr. Burrows, an' that new Butler, Mr. Dalton, he drinks His Lordship's best wine an' lives like a Lord when there's no-one in th' house. Waited on hand-an'-foot, he be! And they say ..."

Mary lowered her voice again.

"They say as he's even sold some o' th' best snuff-boxes, them with the diamonds."

Pandora did not answer.

She was pressing her lips together in case she should say something in front of Mary which she would afterwards regret.

Instead, she dressed almost in silence, only encouraging Mary to go on telling her of the things which had happened on the Estate.

She put on one of the simple but pretty cotton gowns she had brought with her, and arranged her hair as quickly as possible. Then she said to Mary:

"Do not tell anybody that you have spoken to me. Do not answer Mrs. Jenkins back, but just obey orders until I send for you. Do you promise?"

"I promise, Miss Pandora, but Lor', I'd no wish t' get you into trouble."

"I am in enough trouble already for it not to matter to have a little more," Pandora replied, thinking of herself for the first time since the maid had been talking to her.

It struck her suddenly that if the Earl was furious at what she had to say to him, she would find herself in the same position as Mary and her parents.

For the first time the realisation swept over her that she had burnt her bridges.

If her uncle never forgave her for her behaviour in coming here, what would she do?

Now she knew that she had never really believed the stories that her aunt and the ladies in Lindchester had repeated so gleefully about the Earl's behaviour.

Yet now she told herself as she ran down the Great Staircase that she believed every one of them to be true.

There was no sign of the Butler but there were several footmen on duty in the hall.

"Is His Lordship downstairs?" she asked.

"He's in th' Dining-Room, Miss," a footman answered.

"Who else is with him?"

"Two of th' other gentlemen."

"Ask His Lordship to come and speak to me," Pandora ordered.

The footman looked surprised at the tone in which she spoke, but he obeyed her and walked down the corridor to the Dining-Room.

Pandora wondered what she would do if the Earl refused, but a few minutes later he came out of the Dining-Room. As he walked towards her, she saw that he was dressed for riding.

"You are very early ..." he began as he reached her, then saw the expression on her face.

"What is the matter?"

"I have something to say to you of very great importance. Can we go into the Library? We are not likely to be disturbed there."

She spoke as though there was no possibility of his refusing her request, and indeed she had turned to walk towards the Library before he could reply.

They entered the huge room with its walls covered with books, many of them priceless, a unique collection that had been accumulated over the centuries.

The sunshine was pouring in through the long windows and it turned Pandora's hair into what seemed to be a halo of gold.

But her pansy-coloured eyes, so like the Earl's, were dark and angry.

"What has happened? What has upset you?" he asked.

"Do you know what is going on in this house?"

His lips twisted mockingly as he replied:

"I have a good idea."

As if she read his thoughts Pandora said:

"I am not referring to your friends: their behaviour does not concern me. But are you aware that a young housemaid, a girl of sixteen, was ordered by your housekeeper to go to Sir Gilbert's room last night ... or at least I am sure it was Sir Gilbert who ... asked for her."

"What are you talking about?" the Earl asked.

"I am telling you that Mary Clay, whose family I have known all my life, came here two days ago as a housemaid. She is a decent girl and, though she was somewhat nervous about having to work here, they needed the money as your new agent has sacked her father."

"This all seems rather involved."

"It is involved!" Pandora snapped. "But if you will please listen to what I have to say you will understand."

She was shaking not with fear but fury, and the Earl raised his eye-brows as he sat down in one of the red leather arm-chairs and crossed his legs.

"Go on!" he said.

"I have every intention of doing so," Pandora answered, "Mary's grandmother has already been turned out of her cottage to make way for some protégé of Mr. Anstey's. There is no money coming in for the family except what the mother and now Mary are earning, and there are four other children."

Pandora drew in her breath before she continued:

"This girl has been told by your Housekeeper that unless she goes to a certain gentleman's bedroom when he wants her, her whole family will be turned into the street—every one of them!"

Pandora's voice was vibrant with anger, and after a moment the Earl said:

"Can this really be the truth?"

"But of course it is the truth!" Pandora answered. "And while I am not concerned with your friends, these people are mine . . . the people whom Papa loved and looked after, the people who came to my mother with their problems."

Tears welled up in her eyes as she spoke of her mother, but her voice was still angry as she continued:

"Mrs. Meadowfield, who looked after the girls who worked here, has been sent away, and this wicked harridan has been put in her place. I remember you said last night that it was nothing to do with you that Burrows, the former Butler, had gone."

She looked at the Earl as if she expected him to contradict her, then went on:

"Burrows protested because he felt he was one of the family. Count the snuff-boxes now and see how many are missing! The money had gone into your new Butler's pocket, just as Grandpapa's best wines have flowed down the new Butler's throat!"

Pandora paused for breath, then went on:

"I did not believe, could not credit, that the things I had heard about you were true. But they are true! And they are happening at Chart Hall, which is a part of you whether you admit it or not."

Her voice broke as she asked:

"How can you do this? How can you be so cruel ... so insensitive as to ... destroy what those of our blood have ... died to ... preserve?"

Now the tears ran down Pandora's cheeks. She took no heed of them, but merely went on staring at the Earl, the anger still in her eyes, which were so like his.

For a moment he neither moved nor spoke. Then he said in a voice that seemed somehow as tense as hers:

"You have spoken bluntly, Pandora, and I have listened to your accusations. Now perhaps you would like to hear my side of the story."

She did not answer, and he went on:

"Ever since I inherited I have done my best to disgrace the name of Chartwood, and I intend to dissipate or disperse everything this house contains, as I have already begun on the contents of Chartwood House in London."

"But why? Why?" Pandora cried.

"That is what you shall hear," the Earl answered.

He rose to his feet as he spoke, as if it would thus be easier to confront her, and said in a hard voice:

"My father, as you know, was a distant cousin of your grandfather's, and when he was a young man he fell in love with a very beautiful woman. She was ostracised by every member of the Chart family because they called her a 'play-actress.'"

Pandora looked surprised and the Earl went on:

"She was in fact nothing of the sort. She had great musical ability, and because her parents were poverty-stricken she employed the only talent she had to make a living."

He paused to continue angrily:

"She certainly appeared on the stage, and people paid to hear her, and that damned her completely in the eyes of the stuck-up aristocrats."

The Earl walked a few paces across the room and back again, and as Pandora did not speak after a moment he went on:

"My father, shunned by his family, made friends where he could. They were not particularly desirable but at least they amused him while he had money, but he did not have much."

The Earl's voice was bitter and cynical as he continued:

"Then my mother died and he fell ill and nobody wanted him. Least of all the Earl of Chartwood, who, according to you, should have protected the weaker and poorer members of the family."

"What . . . happened?" Pandora asked.

"My father died," the Earl replied, "because I could not raise enough money for him to have an operation which was imperative if he was to live."

"Did you ask Grandpapa to help you?"

"Of course I asked the Almighty Earl of Chartwood—the head of the family—the great father-figure who, like God, was supposed to care for us all!" the Earl retorted violently. "But neither the Earl nor God cared a damn!"

Pandora made a little sound but did not speak.

"My father died in agony and unnecessarily," the Earl went on. "He was still virtually a young man, and the operation was not a very difficult one, but it was absolutely essential if he was to stay alive."

"Are you sure that Grandpapa refused to . . . help you?"

"He wrote me the most charming letter," the Earl answered sarcastically. "He enclosed ten pounds

—*ten pounds*—and told me I would get no more out of him in any circumstances."

He flung himself down in a chair as if he was almost exhausted by the violence with which he had spoken.

"I . . . am sorry . . ." Pandora began to say, then she gave a little cry.

"When did your father die?"

"In 1815."

"After Waterloo!"

"I believe that memorable event happened in the same year," the Earl sneered.

"I remember . . . now I remember exactly what happened," Pandora said, "but of course I had no idea that it was your father."

"What are you talking about?"

"I came in from riding and Mama was talking to Papa. She seemed very upset. 'What has happened, Mama?' I asked.

"'It does not concern you, darling,' she replied, 'but your grandfather was in one of his black moods today. He has been a different man since poor George was killed.'

"'I know that,' I answered.

"Mama looked at my father. 'Charles,' she said, 'I have done a terrible thing.'

"'What have you done?' he enquired.

"'I have stolen five pounds.'

"'Stolen?'

"I could see that even Papa was surprised.

"'Father has received a letter from one of the Chartwood cousins,' Mama explained. 'I do not think I have ever met him, but he wrote to say that his father was desperately ill and needed an operation.'

"She paused as if the memory of the letter upset her, and Papa said sympathetically: 'Go on, darling. I wish you did not have to cope with all these things.'

"'There is no-one else now,' Mama said, and I knew that they were both thinking of Uncle George.

" 'I suggested to Father,' she continued, 'that he should send the cousin the money he needed, but Father would not listen.'

" 'Give him five pounds and tell him to go to the devil!' he said.

"Mama gave a little cry. 'He would never have said anything like that in the old days, but when I tried to argue with him he would not listen.'

" 'So where does your thieving come in?' Papa asked.

" 'You will think it very reprehensible of me,' Mama answered, 'but I took it out of the housekeeping! Father gives me money with which to pay the servants and the bills without asking too many questions. I am sure he will never notice it.'

" 'So you sent your cousin ten pounds?'

" 'Which will not be enough,' Mama said with a sigh. 'Oh, Charles, I wish we were rich. There are so many people I would like to help.'

" 'You do more than enough already,' Papa answered, and kissed her.

" 'It worries me—it really worries me,' she murmured.

" 'If it does that,' Papa replied, 'I will do something about it. Find out the address of your cousin and I will go and see him.'

" 'Would you really, Charles? That would be so kind. I cannot bear to think of him suffering and none of us being able to help.'

" 'Bring me his address,' Papa answered."

Pandora looked at the Earl and saw that he was listening intently.

"If Papa could have found you," she said, "he would—I am sure he would—have found some way to help your father. But I heard Mama tell him the next day that Grandpapa in a temper had thrown the letter in the fire."

She paused.

"I did not think of it until now, but of course he did that because Uncle George had been killed and your father was heir to the title."

She looked at the Earl and went on:

"Mama was very upset because she could not remember your address. She had written a lot of letters that day, and although she tried and tried she could not recall it exactly."

The Earl did not speak and Pandora continued:

"Even so, as she was sure it was somewhere in Islington, Papa spent a whole day in the neighbourhood, but no-one had heard of a householder by the name of Chart!"

"That was not surprising, as we were staying in a cheap boarding-house," the Earl said bitterly.

He rose from his chair and walked across the room to stand at one of the windows looking out onto the garden.

"I have hated your grandfather so violently that it has poisoned my whole outlook on life," he said, "but I did not realise until after my father was dead that he had been in fact the heir for three months."

"Then you . . . knew it had . . . come to . . . you."

"I borrowed money on the strength of it," the Earl said with a defiant note in his voice, "not much, because Money-Lenders are not over generous to heir presumptives, but enough to give me a taste of the life that was to be mine once I became the fifth Earl and inherited not only a coronet but a fortune!"

Pandora did not speak.

She suddenly felt that her anger had gone from her and she felt instead deflated and at the same time a little weak.

"I am . . . sorry I was so . . . rude," she said after a moment. "I lost my temper, and I know it was wrong of Grandpapa to behave as he did, but it was in fact very unlike him."

"I suppose we can both understand that he hated me just as I hated him!" the Earl said.

"He adored his sons," Pandora went on as if the Earl had not spoken. "I suppose every man wants a son to carry on his name. I know Papa, although he loved me, would have liked a boy, and he always hoped he would have a son. But the Doctors said it would be a miracle if Mama ever had another child."

She spoke a little sadly, then she said:

"But you must have lots of children. I used to think when I came here as a little girl what fun it would be if there were other children to slide down the Long Gallery and play hide-and-seek in the Orangery."

"I have decided not to perpetuate the name of Chartwood," the Earl answered abruptly.

"How can you be so ridiculous?" Pandora asked, the softness swept away from her voice. "As I said last night, you have been so lucky, but instead of being grateful you are letting what happened in the past destroy your judgement and ruin your own life."

"Do you really think it is ruined?" the Earl asked.

"Well, you cannot go on forever being amused by . . ."

Pandora stopped because she thought she was being rude.

"Go on," the Earl said. "Let me hear what you think of my friends—the only friends I have."

"I just wonder how long they would stay your friends if you had no money," Pandora snapped.

For a moment the Earl glared at her, then he laughed.

"You are certainly frank, my saintly little cousin. Leave me to my sins—I prefer it that way."

"You can sin as much as you like," Pandora said, "and I would make no attempt to stop you, but you cannot force a young girl like Mary to be corrupted by that . . . horrible . . . beastly man who came to . . . my bed-room last . . . night!"

She gave a little shiver.

"I was thinking when he had gone how fortunate it was that you were there to save me . . . and how . . . kind you . . . were."

She paused and her voice softened as she said:

"I went to sleep thinking you were not . . . as bad as you . . . pretend to be—but now I am not . . . sure."

"That is deliberately inviting me to say that I

will show you that I am not only as bad as you think I am, but very much worse!"

"And will that give you any great satisfaction?" Pandora asked. "When you have left everyone here weeping, miserable, and starving, what will you have proved? That you can be cruel, hard, and wicked? Well, I dare say the family has survived men like you before."

She glared at him as she continued:

"There was one Chart who joined the Round-heads and treacherously denounced the hiding-place of his brother, who was a Royalist. There was another who shot himself after he had lost so much money at cards that he could not meet his debts, without selling the family treasures."

She paused before she added:

"They mattered to him more than life, and I dare say if you go through the history-books you would find a dozen more, and I hope you enjoy their company!"

She turned as she spoke and walked towards the door.

"Where are you going?" the Earl asked.

"I am going back to Lindchester and taking the Clay family with me. Because I think it is unlikely that my uncle will ever forgive me or help them, I am going on my knees to everyone who is kind and charitable."

Her voice rose as she added:

"There must be a heart somewhere, even amongst those whom you sneer at as 'sanctimonious.'"

Her hand was on the door when the Earl said:

"Come here, you little spitfire!"

She did not obey him, but she did not leave the room.

"I suppose anyone would know we are relations," the Earl said. "We have the same bald-headed way of going about things."

Pandora took a step towards him.

"You will save Mary Clay?"

The Earl did not speak for a moment. Then he said:

"I suppose there is no reason why the sins of the father should be visited upon the pensioners."

Pandora ran across the room towards him.

"What are you . . . saying?" she asked. "Explain it to me . . . simply."

He looked down at her, at the pleading in her eyes as they searched his.

"Do you know," he asked after a moment, "where the previous Housekeeper—what was her name?—Mrs. Meadowfield? Do you know where she is living?"

"Oh, yes!" Pandora said breathlessly.

"And Burrows, the former Butler? I remember him when I first came here."

"He lives in the village."

"Are you prepared to go and fetch them back?"

"Oh, Cousin Norvin! Do you mean that?"

The tears were back in Pandora's eyes, but now they seemed to glitter like stars.

"You will remember I offered you *Paradise Regained?*"

"That is exactly what you are doing," Pandora said breathlessly. "And what about . . . Mr. Anstey?"

"What about him?" the Earl asked in an uncompromising voice.

"Mr. Farrow, whom everybody loved, was, I think, glad to retire, but his son, Michael, knows everything about the Estate. He worked with him during the last few years and he will know how to put everything right."

She was begging him to understand as she said:

"You will not be troubled, you will not be worried, but things will be as they were when I first came here as a child; and it was all so . . . wonderful, like a King's Palace in a . . . fairy-story."

"Very well then," the Earl said. "You are determined to have your own way. Tell Farrow to call on me in two hours' time."

He smiled rather cynically as he added:

"You had better hurry or I may change my mind! Anyway, there is going to be a row, and if you do not wish to be involved in it, get out of the house!"

"I cannot believe it. It is all so wonderful! Oh, Cousin Norvin, I knew that you were only pretending to be bad."

"You are white-washing me and it will not stick," the Earl replied.

"I am giving you a halo," Pandora flashed, "and do not let it slip!"

She ran across the room and only as she reached the door did she look back over her shoulder.

"Please count the snuff-boxes," she said. "They are very precious."

She heard the Earl laugh as she ran down the corridor.

She tore up to her room and rang the bell for Mary.

Before the maid came she had put on a bonnet and was searching the drawers for her gloves.

"Yes, Miss?" Mary said from the doorway.

"It is all right, Mary! Everything is all right!" Pandora cried. "But do not say a word to anyone yet. Just wait! It is going to be exactly the same as when Grandpapa was here, and everybody will be happy."

"You can't mean it, Miss!"

Pandora found her gloves.

"Do not even breathe a word of this to your mother," she said. "Just behave as usual until I return."

There was an expression of hope in Mary's face as she passed her and ran down the stairs to the hall.

There was still no sign of Dalton, for which she was grateful, but to one of the footmen she said:

"I want a carriage to drive to the village, and as it is such a lovely day I will start walking down the drive. Will you tell the coachman to catch me up as quickly as possible?"

"Very good, Miss."

Pandora walked out through the front door and into the sunshine.

The Earl had told her to hurry and she wanted to get away just in case there were any alterations to his orders. She also had no wish to meet any of the members of the house-party.

Her heart was singing and she was so excited that she wanted to dance rather than walk, but she forced herself to move sedately towards the lake and over the old stone bridge.

Now there was park-land on either side of her with its speckled deer, which because she used to feed them became quite tame. And there were oak trees with their branches almost meeting across the drive to form a green tunnel.

When she had walked for a little way she turned to look back.

The Castle was majestic in the sunshine, but to Pandora it was as if the light on the windows made it smile at her with a new happiness.

It suddenly struck her that it was Chart Hall that had won the battle, not herself. It had survived so many ups and downs during the long years it had stood there.

Religious Wars and Civil Wars had raged round it; there had been Charts who were spend-thrifts and Charts who were misers; but the Hall itself had always survived.

Perhaps, she thought, it had become the controlling influence in the life of every member of the family wherever he or she might be.

One action on the part of her grandfather had made the present Earl seek to revenge himself violently, not on the man who was dead but on the house that had been his background and an intrinsic part of the family.

'Chart Hall has proved too strong for him!' Pandora reproved.

Even if she had not accelerated things by raging at him at this particular moment, she could not help feeling that sooner or later the Castle itself would have spoken to him, enveloped him, and protected him, as it were, against himself.

"You are always there in our lives," she said to it now.

Then she saw the carriage coming towards her.

*   *   *

She went first to find Michael Farrow.

She knew that his father had a house on the outskirts of the village, and as the carriage stopped beside the gate, which was too small for the horses to pass through, she saw Michael, whom she had known ever since she was a child, digging in the garden.

As she waved to him he put down his spade and came to meet her with a look of surprise on his face.

"I wondered who could be calling, Miss Pandora," he said. "But surely that's one of the carriages from the Hall?"

"I have come to see you and your father," Pandora answered.

"Father will be delighted to see you. He so often talks of your mother. He always says she was the most beautiful person he ever knew."

"That is what I thought," Pandora said, smiling.

"If you want to talk to me," Michael Farrow said, "you'll have to excuse me while I wash my hands. We can't afford a gardener these days, so I have to do the digging myself."

It struck Pandora that Mr. Farrow had very likely been dismissed without an adequate pension. That did not matter now, although she knew that it was a grave injustice after his long years of service to the Estate.

Mr. Farrow, who seemed to have grown very old suddenly, was sitting in the front room of his house, reading the newspaper.

He put it down to stare at Pandora in astonishment before he rose with some difficulty to his feet.

"Do not get up," Pandora begged.

"I am having trouble with my legs these days," Mr. Farrow answered. "It is due to lack of exercise, I think. I used to do so much riding when I was up at the Hall, but I find myself now getting chair-bound."

He tried to laugh, but the sadness in his face was very apparent.

"It is nice to see you again," Pandora said.

"I miss your father and mother more than I can ever tell you," Mr. Farrow said, "and the village misses them too. Things are not what they used to be."

"That is what I have come to talk to you about," Pandora said.

Mr. Farrow looked at her enquiringly as Michael came into the room.

She told him briefly that the Earl had decided Mr. Anstey was not satisfactory. She had suggested that Michael Farrow should take over the Estate, and she was sure that his father would want to help him until he found his feet.

For a moment the two men stared at her as if she had taken leave of her senses. Then Mr. Farrow said quietly:

"Are you telling me that His Lordship intends to dispense with the services of Mr. Anstey altogether?"

"I am hoping and praying that he will have left by the time Michael reaches the Hall," Pandora answered. "His Lordship said he would see him in two hours' time, and it must be an hour and a half by now."

She did not wait to listen to their thanks, but hurried away to stop at the cottage where she knew she would find Mrs. Meadowfield.

It was where her sister lived who had been the school-teacher for many years until she retired.

Mrs. Meadowfield was grey-haired but full of energy and she greeted Pandora excitedly.

"It's like a breath of fresh air to see you again, Miss," she said. "I was talking about your dear mother and father only yesterday. There's not a person in the village as doesn't shed a tear when they speaks of them."

"I have come to ask you, Mrs. Meadowfield," Pandora said, "if you will come back with me immediately to the Hall."

"Back to the Hall?" Mrs. Meadowfield enquired. "What for?"

"The household needs you—needs you badly!" Pandora replied. "There will be plenty of people to tell you what has been happening, so I do not intend to do so."

"You mean that His Lordship has asked for me to come back to my old position?" Mrs. Meadowfield asked. "Well, after the way I was treated, Miss Pandora..."

Pandora put out her hand and laid it on the old woman's arm.

"Please, Mrs. Meadowfield," she interrupted, "come with me. You are the only person who can put things right, which is something which has to be done, and at once!"

The words of affronted dignity which Mrs. Meadowfield was about to utter died on her lips. She looked into Pandora's face and said:

"You're just like your mother, dear, and I never could refuse anything she asked of me."

Pandora gave her time only to get her hat and cloak.

"I am sure your sister will pack your box," she said, "and you can send for it later this afternoon."

It was only a very short distance to the cottage to which Mr. Burrows had retired.

It was not far from the Vicarage, and as Pandora passed first the Church and then the house where she had been so happy with her parents, she found herself thinking that her father and mother had helped her to set things right at the Hall.

It would have hurt both of them to know what was going on and to find that their friends in the village had been unjustly treated, or, worse still, that girls like Mary might have been corrupted and led astray.

'If that had actually happened,' Pandora thought to herself, 'Prosper Witheridge would have been justified in all his accusations.'

It was only when she was driving back, with

Mrs. Meadowfield sitting beside her and old Burrows opposite, both of them too surprised to have
much to say, that she remembered that there was
still the house-party to contend with.

She knew that Mrs. Meadowfield would be
deeply shocked at the way the actresses behaved
and spoke, and she thought old Burrows would be
appalled if the best china dishes were broken at the
table or anyone dented the silver.

Then she told herself that she was quite certain
he would have the good sense not to use the best
table-ware.

He knew far better than the present owner of
the house what they were, and she deliberately
stopped herself from asking him to take care and to
prevent from happening again the sort of incident
that had taken place last night.

Because she knew they would expect it, she told
the coachman to pull up at the side of the house so
that Mrs. Meadowfield and Burrows could walk round
to the back entrance.

Then she drove up to the front and knew as
soon as she saw the expressions on the faces of the
footmen that things had been happening.

She had been longer than she had expected. It
was in fact nearly luncheon-time and she realised that
she was very hungry.

Mary's revelations had prevented her from having any breakfast and it seemed a long time since
dinner the preceding evening.

She walked into the hall, saw a hat lying on a
chair, and knew that Michael Farrow had arrived and
was doubtless with the Earl.

She went upstairs to her bed-room and as she
was taking off her bonnet Mary came in.

"Oh, Miss Pandora, such goings-on! Such excitement as you never knowed!" Mary exclaimed.

"What has been happening?" Pandora asked with
a smile.

"Almost immediately after you'd gone, his Lordship sends for Mrs. Jenkins and Mr. Dalton. He sacks

them both, an' I hear from one of the footmen that they were very impudent in the things they says to him!"

Mary paused before she went on with relish:

"James says as His Lordship was looking black as thunder when he sees Mr. Anstey."

"What happened then?" Pandora asked.

"You'll never believe, Miss, but when Mr. Anstey rides off out the front door he shakes his fist at him! 'You'll rue this day!' he says. 'Mark my words—you'll all of you rue this day!'"

Pandora gave a sigh of relief.

The Earl had kept his word. Mr. Anstey had gone, and she could only hope that all the outsiders whom he had put into the cottages on the Estate would follow him.

Mary was almost incoherent with excitement, but she had very little more to tell.

Demurely Pandora went downstairs to the Salon, and found only Hettie there, looking very hollow-eyed and talking with Freddie and Clive.

"It must be nearly luncheon-time," Pandora said as the two gentlemen rose. "Where is everybody?"

"All too ill to appear," Hettie answered. "Caro has been sick all night and so has Lottie. Kitty's got such a headache that she can't open her eyes."

"The trouble with Norvin's wines," Freddie said, "is that they are too good and too heavy. If the girls had taken my advice and stuck to champagne, they would have been all right!"

"That comes well from you!" Hettie replied. "You were completely bosky, as you well know, and Richard was as tight as a Lord."

"That reminds me, I have not seen our host this morning," Clive said. "I thought he was coming riding with us."

"I think he had other things to do," Pandora said.

"Well, if he did them with you," Hettie remarked, "Kitty will scratch your eyes out. I'm warning you, she's very jealous, and she doesn't talk—she acts!"

"There is no reason for Kitty to be jealous of me," Pandora answered. "I am just the poor relation and nobody ever worries about them!"

The two men laughed and Hettie said:

"Well, don't say I didn't warn you!"

The Earl appeared, and looking at him Pandora knew without being told that he had enjoyed himself.

She had the feeling that he liked getting his teeth into something difficult.

It was characteristic of many of the Charts and she thought that perhaps one of his troubles was that since he had inherited a great fortune he had had nothing more arduous to do than to be entertained.

Her mother had always said that men were at their best when they were doing something.

"They are like children," she had said. "When a child asks: 'What shall I do?' you know they are bored, and that is when they get into mischief."

"Where have you been all the morning?" Freddie asked as the Earl joined them. "Clive and I felt better after a gallop on your excellent horses, but it does not look as though you have sat on anything except a chair."

"I have been rather busy with affairs concerning the house and the Estate," the Earl replied.

He looked at Pandora as he spoke and his eyes were twinkling.

Without really thinking what she was doing, she slipped her hand into his.

"It has been very exciting!" she said in a low voice.

The Earl's fingers squeezed hers and only as she saw the suspicious look on Hettie's face did she wonder if she had been indiscreet.

Chapter Four

When luncheon was over the Earl rose to his feet and said:

"I am going riding."

He had eaten very little and Pandora was sure that his mind was on other things.

He certainly paid very little attention to what Hettie was saying, and he answered his friends absent-mindedly.

She had been relieved to find that there was no sign of Sir Gilbert.

Although she did not ask about him, Richard told her what she wanted to know when he mentioned that last night Sir Gilbert had made an arrangement to see Sir Edward Trentham today.

Clive and Richard now looked at the Earl enquiringly as if they expected him to invite them to ride with him, but before they could speak the Earl said:

"If you are not too tired, Pandora, I would like you to come with me. There are things I want to see which I feel only you can show me."

"Of course, Cousin Norvin."

She hurried excitedly upstairs to change into a riding-habit. She had put one in her trunk with the faint hope that there would be a chance of her riding again over the land she loved.

Because she knew that men hated to be kept waiting, she pulled off her gown and hurried into the pretty green habit that she had worn for several years but which still fitted her.

It might be old, but it was well cut.

However much they economised on their ordinary gowns, her father had always insisted that she and her mother were properly dressed in the hunting-field.

Arranging her hair in a chignon at the back of her head, she put on the high-crowned hat she wore for riding, which had a gauze veil of the same colour as her habit to float out behind it.

Then she ran downstairs to find the Earl waiting for her in the hall, and outside were two magnificent horses, better bred than anything she had ever before ridden or her father could have afforded to buy.

The Earl lifted her into the saddle, and as his hands went to either side of her small waist she realised how strong he was.

She looked down at him, met his eyes, and what she had been about to say suddenly left her mind. She knew only that he was smiling and that some of the lines seemed to have gone from his face.

He looked up at her for what seemed to be a long time, but could in fact have been only a few seconds, before he turned and mounted his own horse.

Pandora supposed it must be the excitement of riding again at Chart, but her heart was beating in a strange manner and she felt as if it was hard to breathe.

They had reached the bridge before she managed to say:

"Where do you wish to go?"

"I thought you might like to show me the part of the Estate I have not yet seen," the Earl answered.

"What have you seen already?"

"Very little," he admitted. "At Christmastime the weather was bad and we were all excessively drunk. The last time I was here I spent my time with a fair charmer who did not ride."

Pandora had the idea that he was deliberately saying such things because he thought they would shock her.

They were duelling with each other, she thought, not only in words but as if they were well-matched fencers and every move was calculated.

"Then I will show you the farms," she said, "and tell you a little about the men who run them for you. I suppose you know that you have two thousand acres in hand. The rest is let to tenant-farmers who have been with us for many years."

She realised as she spoke that she was identifying herself with Chart, then silently asked herself, 'Why not?'

She was as much a part of it as he was, except that he had the power and—if he wished it—the glory.

They rode to the largest farm, which was let to a family who had lived there ever since she could remember.

There were four sons, who did the majority of the work as their father was getting old, and they were now out in the fields.

The father was feeding some new-born calves and his wife was feeding a flock of geese and collecting the eggs.

As soon as Pandora appeared they greeted her effusively, but when she introduced them to the Earl there was a cold silence and they looked at him apprehensively.

"If ye've come t' turn me out, M'Lord," the farmer said, "there's nought Oi can do about it. Ye've bled us white this last six months, an' the only way Oi can pay what Oi owes is to sell me stock, an' that, as any farmer knows, be the beginning of the end!"

"Are you referring to the rent?" the Earl enquired.

"What else?" the farmer asked aggressively.

"How much more are you paying since I inherited than you paid before?"

The farmer looked at him incredulously.

"Oi understood as the rises were directly on Ye Lordship's orders."

"Then you were mistaken!" the Earl said sharply.

"Tell His Lordship the difference," Pandora said softly.

"Over twice as much, M'Lord, an' we've been told that ten percent of everythin' we sells at the market has to be given to Ye Lordship."

Pandora gasped.

She knew this was exorbitant to say the least of it, and she wondered if the Earl would understand that it would be impossible for any farmer to meet such demands honestly.

It seemed to her that there was a long silence before the Earl said:

"There has obviously been some mistake. You will pay in rent exactly what you used to pay in the past, and your sales do not concern me and are the reward you receive for your labour."

The incredulous expression on the farmer's face made Pandora feel that she wanted to cry.

"D-do ye mean th-that, M'Lord?" the old man managed to stammer.

"My new manager, Mr. Michael Farrow, will, I am sure, explain to you that what has been happening recently has not been on my instructions."

"Oi canna believe it!" the farmer said slowly. "Thank ye, M'Lord, thank ye! Ye've taken a load off me shoulders, an' the Missus'll sleep sound again at night."

They insisted on Pandora and the Earl going into the farm-house to drink a glass of their home-brewed cider and eat a slice of their home-cured ham.

Pandora was glad to see that the Earl was very much at his ease with these simple people.

Although the farmer's wife had burst into tears when she was first told the good news, she dried them quickly and was all smiles and happiness when finally they left.

"God bless ye, Miss Pandora," she added as they

said good-bye. "This be a happy day for us and Oi knows as how yer father, God bless him, would rejoice to know that things up at th' Hall are going to be as they was."

"I am sure he would," Pandora said softly.

She and the Earl rode away, and when they reached the next farm almost the identical scene took place.

She had a feeling that now the Earl was positively enjoying himself.

She was perceptive enough to realise that after years of poverty it was pleasant for him to feel that he was in the seat of power and his people relied on him.

That was the right word, she thought, and as they rode on again she said:

"Now you understand, I think, how important the Earl of Chartwood is! Not only in London in attendance upon the King, but here where you reign supreme."

"I shall become conceited and very puffed up with my own importance if you talk to me like that," the Earl replied.

"What I am saying is true," Pandora said. "Papa said once that Chart is like a State within a State. You see, we are almost self-sufficient. There are not only farmers, but stone-masons, wood-cutters, carpenters, iron-workers, and smithies, and of course all the offices which directly serve the house."

"I have seen none of these places," the Earl replied. "I am quite certain you will have something scathing to say about my negligence."

"I am prepared to accept it as ignorance," Pandora said teasingly.

"Well, Miss Know-All, this is your glorious hour," he replied. "I will allow you to bully me for the moment, but I have always fancied myself as being an efficient organiser, so once you have served your purpose I shall have no further use for you!"

Pandora knew he was joking in the spirit in which she had teased him, but she felt as they turned for home that there was many a true word spoken in jest.

They had seen only a tenth of what there was to be seen, and yet she realised he was grasping the organisation of the great Estate with an intelligence and a capacity to learn that she would not have expected of him.

He asked extremely pertinent questions not only of her but of the farmers and the other people they met, and as they rode back through the village he looked at the Vicarage and said:

"I wish your father were still here. I am sure he would be able to tell me a great many other things I want to know."

"What sort of things?" Pandora asked, curious.

"About the people themselves, the men of the village, the sort of lives they lead when they are not at work. Do you think it would seem strange if I went to the Inn and ordered myself a drink?"

Pandora smiled.

"I think Mr. Tubb, who keeps the Dog and Fox, would be delighted if you called on him. He has been there for twenty-five years and his father kept it before him."

"Very well, I will go there tomorrow," the Earl said. "I cannot believe that an Inn is the sort of place that you could visit."

Pandora laughed.

"You are not in London now and I assure you that the Dog and Fox is very respectable."

Because she thought he looked surprised, she added:

"Of course I would not be allowed to enter an Inn or what they call a 'Public House' in Lindchester. Uncle Augustus would have a stroke at the idea!"

She laughed again and went on:

"But Mrs. Tubb always had a glass of apple-juice for me when I was a little girl, and actually Mr. Tubb would never serve anyone who had over-indulged. So drunkenness in Chart village is very, very rare."

"Rather different from Chart Hall," the Earl remarked dryly.

Pandora did not reply for a moment. Then she said:

"You will think it very ignorant of me, but I cannot understand why anyone wants to drink so much that they are ill the next day. It seems such a waste when life is so short."

"You talk as though you were an octogenarian," the Earl replied. "You have long years ahead of you."

"It is not long enough to do all the things I want to do," Pandora said, and gave a little sigh. "If I had the . . . chance."

"What do you want to do?"

"Read, for one thing; travel, for another; and see Chart as it used to be in all its glory."

"Is it not glorious enough for you now?"

"Not really," Pandora answered. "You see, the people who work for the house want appreciation even more than the owner of it. It is no use for the gardeners to grow beautiful flowers and magnificent fruit if there is nobody to enjoy them."

She glanced at the Earl under her eye-lashes and continued:

"The horses get fat and lazy in the stables because there is no point in exercising them if they are not going to be ridden by somebody who really appreciates how fit they are."

"Are you seriously suggesting that I should live at Chart?" the Earl asked.

"Why not? Grandpapa when he was young used to be at Chart for nine months of the year. It was lovely in the summer, and there was shooting and hunting in the autumn. If it had not been for the war, he always said, he would have gone to Rome or to the South of France in the spring."

The Earl did not speak and after a pause Pandora went on:

"Chart House in London was opened for the Season. That was all, but there was a magnificent party given in the Ball-Room when Mama made her début. She often told me about it."

"And that is what you would have liked for yourself," the Earl said.

"Shall I tell you how I spent my eighteenth birthday?" Pandora asked.

"Tell me."

"I spent the morning delivering religious tracts to some old women in the Alms-Houses who did not want them but were quite glad to have a chat."

The Earl gave a little laugh and she went on:

"In the afternoon my aunt was extremely angry because I had not washed some table-cloths as well as she would have wished. She made me do them again twice as a punishment, deliberately rubbing soot into them after I had spent an hour pressing them with a hot iron."

Pandora drew in her breath.

"It was rather different from being given a Ball at . . . Chart House."

Her voice cracked on the last word and she spurred her horse forward so that the Earl should not see the tears which gathered in her eyes.

She told herself a moment later that she should not have complained to him.

She had not really meant to, but it was hard sometimes, especially when she was at Chart, not to resent the misery and unhappiness that living with her uncle and aunt had brought her.

After they had visited the Mill where their own grain was ground, the Earl said reluctantly:

"I suppose we ought to go back."

Pandora had forgotten the time and now she asked:

"How late is it?"

"Nearly a quarter after five."

"So late?" she exclaimed. "I have not shown you half the things I meant to."

"There is always tomorrow," he answered.

"Yes, of course," Pandora said, and it was an expression of relief.

There were still two days before her uncle and aunt returned, at which time she supposed she would have to go back to Lindchester.

"I had no idea until Farrow told me," the Earl said as they turned their horses towards the great house, "how many people I employ."

He was speaking reflectively and after a moment Pandora said:

"I will not say the obvious."

"But you are thinking it. You are thinking that I am the wrong person to be here simply because I have not shown myself to be interested enough to find these things out before."

"I was not thinking that at all," Pandora contradicted.

"Then tell me what you were thinking."

"Do you want the truth?"

"Yes."

"I was thinking that it was useless for you to fight Chart, which will capture you, hold you, and entrance you, because it is not only so beautiful but also so interesting. There are so many things that need to be done."

"What sort of things?"

"New houses to be built, new quarries to be opened, other parts of the land to be cultivated. Papa used to say that after Uncle George died, Grandpapa let things go. And even in four years things can get out-of-date, and go backwards instead of forwards."

"I understand what you are trying to say," the Earl said. "And what would your answer be if I told you I prefer my riotous, dissolute life in the gaiety of London?"

He spoke aggressively, but Pandora knew that he was fencing with her again.

She looked at him and realised that he not only rode well but looked part of his horse.

"There is a parable in the Bible," she replied after a moment, "about the Prodigal Son."

"But he was eating husks and sitting amongst swine," the Earl replied.

"You must know by now what sort of companions they make," Pandora answered provocatively.

"If you are speaking of my friends," the Earl replied, "I think I shall beat you. It is certainly what you deserve!"

She had anticipated what his reaction would be, and now she laughed at him over her shoulder and touched her horse with her whip, galloping away from him at a wild pace.

They crossed the park, the Earl trying vainly to catch up with her, and only as they reached the stone bridge did Pandora draw in her horse and wait for him to come to her side.

"I won!" she cried. "So you must be ... magnanimous and ... forgive me."

She spoke a little breathlessly.

"I will let you off this time," the Earl said, "but be careful, Pandora, and remember that I am a dark Chart and have a temper."

She laughed again as they rode side by side over the bridge.

"Are you a fisherman?" she asked, looking down at the silvery water.

"I used to be," he replied, "and rather fancied myself a good one."

"Then if you are very good," Pandora promised, "I will show you where Papa used to catch the most delicious brown trout."

"Perhaps we could have a picnic," the Earl said, "and to show you how good I am, we will rely for our meal on the trout I catch."

"It would be very ignominious if we came home hungry," Pandora remarked.

"If the trout are there, I promise you we will not!" the Earl said confidently.

The grooms were waiting for them at the front door, and as Pandora dismounted she thought what fun such a picnic would be.

Then it suddenly struck her that the Earl might bring Kitty and the others with him.

She had almost forgotten that there was anyone

else staying at Chart Hall, until as she went up the stairs to change her clothes she heard voices and laughter coming from the Salon.

She changed into one of her simple after-noon-gowns and when she came downstairs it was to find that the rest of the party were already drink-ing and Kitty and Caro were amongst them.

The actresses were all gowned in silks and gauzes in brilliant colours, flashing with jewellery, the make-up on their faces hiding the ravages of their over-indulgence of the night before.

They were very noisy but as Pandora came into the Salon Kitty asked aggressively:

"Where the hell have you been all this time? I heard you'd gone out riding with my young man."

"I have been showing my cousin some of the Estate," Pandora replied, "and I am afraid we forgot the time; there were so many people for him to see."

"And so much for you to say to him, no doubt," Kitty said sourly.

Burrows had followed Pandora into the Salon and now he asked:

"Would you like some tea, Miss Pandora?"

"I would indeed," Pandora answered. "Thank you, Burrows, for thinking of it."

She saw that behind him were two footmen carrying in a silver tray on which there was the beautiful Queen Anne tea-pot and the milk and sugar basins which had always been used in her mother's time.

There were the sandwiches, fairy-cakes, and other delicacies that were traditional, and as they were set down in front of an arm-chair, Pandora, looking at Hettie and Caro, asked:

"Would anyone else like tea?"

"Who wants tea when you can have cham-pagne?" Caro replied scornfully.

"I should like some," Sir Gilbert said, deliber-ately putting down his glass and coming to stand be-side the tea-table.

"Milk and sugar?" Pandora asked politely, pouring it out for him.

She knew he was staring at her in the manner she most disliked, and she deliberately looked away as she handed him his cup of tea.

"I was afraid you might have left," he said in a low voice, seating himself beside her. "I was reassured when I learnt you had only gone riding."

"I cannot see why it should interest you particularly," Pandora remarked unwisely.

"Then I will tell you why," he said, "but it would be easier to do so if we were alone."

She did not answer but busied herself with pouring out her own tea.

She also took one of the sandwiches, still keeping her head turned as far away as she could from Sir Gilbert.

"You are very lovely!" he said. "And I should like to have seen you on a horse. If I had known that you could ride, I would have refused Trentham's invitation and stayed here."

"My cousin and I had business to attend to," Pandora said coldly.

"Well, now you are free," Sir Gilbert said, "and you can attend to me."

"I think it will soon be time to change for dinner."

"Come and show me the Picture Gallery, for I have never seen it before."

"There will not be time."

"You are being very elusive," Sir Gilbert said, "but I assure you I am a very determined hunter and a very successful one."

Pandora told herself she should not be drawn into such a conversation, but she knew he deliberately gave everything he said an ulterior meaning.

Instead she finished her sandwich and drank her tea without speaking, vividly conscious of the man sitting next to her.

Then, to her relief, the Earl came into the Salon.

The women gave a scream of delight at the

sight of him, but he ignored them and as he walked across the room towards Pandora she saw that he carried something in his hand.

It was a silk handkerchief and it contained something heavy, which he put down in her lap.

She looked at him in surprise as he said:

"You were quite right—Farrow found them. He insisted upon searching Dalton's luggage before he left the house."

Pandora opened the handkerchief. Inside were four snuff-boxes.

She gave a little cry of sheer delight.

"There are several others missing," the Earl said, "but Dalton has confessed where he sold them and Farrow thinks he can get them back."

"Oh, I am glad!" Pandora exclaimed.

She held up one of the snuff-boxes.

"Do you realise this was given by Peter the Great to our ancestor who was the Ambassador to Saint Petersburg? I should have been miserable if it had been lost."

The Earl was about to say something when there was an interruption.

"Why the hell are you giving her presents?" Kitty asked furiously.

She looked at the snuff-box in Pandora's hand and cried:

"And diamonds too! If there's any diamonds to be had, I'm having them, and make no mistake about it."

She would have snatched the box from Pandora's hand but the Earl put out his arm and prevented her.

"They are not a present for Pandora," he said coldly. "They belong to the house, but were stolen by one of the servants."

"You expect me to believe that nonsense?" Kitty asked. "And even if it's true—give them to me!"

"They are of no use to you," the Earl said good-humoredly. "You cannot wear them round your neck or in your ears."

"They contain diamonds, which can be reset," Kitty exclaimed furiously.

Pandora laid the snuff-box back in the handkerchief with the others and rose to her feet.

"I will put them back in their proper places," she said.

"Oh no you won't!" Kitty screamed.

Now she escaped the Earl's restraining arm and flew at Pandora.

She took her by surprise and as she pushed at her in an effort to snatch the weighted handkerchief, Pandora stumbled and would have fallen if to her consternation Sir Gilbert had not prevented her from doing so.

"That is enough, Kitty!" the Earl said angrily. "Behave yourself! I have told you—the snuff-boxes belong to my house and nobody is going to remove them from it."

He spoke forcibly in a way that surprised both Kitty and Pandora.

Pandora tried to disengage herself from the overly protective arms of Sir Gilbert.

"Thank you," she said. "I am quite all right now."

"I am prepared to hold you as long as is necessary."

"It is unnecessary," she replied.

The Earl, grappling with Kitty, suddenly seemed to realise what was happening.

"Let her go, Gilbert," he said. "And the sooner the snuff-boxes are in their proper places, the better!"

Reluctantly Sir Gilbert took his arms from Pandora.

"You are adorably soft to hold," he said softly against her ear.

She walked to the end of the room to set two of the snuff-boxes down on a Louis XIV table. Then, without looking round, she walked quickly from the room, shutting the door behind her.

The two other snuff-boxes came from the Library, and when she put them back she saw, as she had feared, that three others were missing, all very valuable ones set with precious stones and emblazoned with enamel-work.

"What we must have here is another Curator," she said to herself.

The previous Curator had died about three years ago and had never been replaced, but she knew that his catalogue of the contents of the house would be in the desk that he had always used in the Estate office.

She thought she would ask Michael Farrow tomorrow if he could think of anyone who was prepared to take up such a position.

Then she told herself that that would be a mistake.

She would be interfering.

She tried to think of what her mother would have done, and she knew that she must try to put the idea into the Earl's head that a Curator was necessary. But the suggestion of finding one must come from him.

"If I am to help him I must be clever about it," Pandora told herself. "Men hate bossy women, and once he wants to run the house himself he will resent my interference or anyone else's."

It was one thing to think things out logically and calmly, and quite another not to feel that it was a question of time.

The sands were running out and soon the retribution which hung over her head like the sword of Damocles would fall, when her uncle returned to Lindchester on Friday.

'There are still two days,' she thought with an irrepressible feeling of joy, and she determined to make use of every minute of those days.

She ran upstairs to find Mary almost hysterical with happiness.

"Things are ever so different already, Miss," she said. "From the moment Mrs. Meadowfield arrived, everything began t' change."

"I thought it would," Pandora said with a smile.

"Two of the housemaids left with Mrs. Jenkins because they'd come with her," Mary went on. "We're short-handed but the rest of us will work our fingers t' the bone, that we will, Miss, t' make things as they ought t' be."

While Pandora was dressing, Mrs. Meadowfield came to see her.

"You have everything you want, Miss Pandora?" she asked.

"Yes, thank you, Mrs. Meadowfield," Pandora answered. "It is so delightful to have you here."

Mrs. Meadowfield smiled her appreciation. She was wearing the black gown with its taffeta apron that Pandora remembered, and the silver chatelaine with its clanking keys hung from her waist.

She sent Mary on an errand and when the girl was gone she said to Pandora:

"I've never seen anything like the mess everything's in, Miss Pandora. I don't know what your mother would have said, I don't really! The linen's all topsy-turvy, the rooms aren't properly spring-cleaned, and a lot of things are broken or missing."

"I am sure you will soon put everything right again," Pandora said.

"I hopes so, Miss. His Lordship shouldn't be using the State Bed-Rooms for—"

She stopped suddenly, but Pandora was well aware of what she had been about to say.

"We have to help His Lordship, Mrs. Meadowfield," she said. "It takes a long time to know Chart in the way you and I know it. He wants to learn, but since he is a man we must not push him too hard at first."

"You're as wise as your mother was, Miss Pandora," Mrs. Meadowfield replied. "Many's the time she said to me about your grandfather: 'Let His Lordship think it's his idea, Mrs. Meadowfield,' and that's exactly what I done."

"And that is what you must do again," Pandora said.

Mrs. Meadowfield looked round the room to see that everything was in order. Then she said:

"It's here you belong, Miss Pandora, and that's a fact. I've often said to my sister: 'It's not right Miss Pandora should be at Lindchester when her home's here, so to speak.'"

Pandora kissed Mrs. Meadowfield on the cheek.

"That is what Chart Hall, Chart village, and you will always be to me," she said, "home!"

She went downstairs to find that because she had stopped to talk to Mrs. Meadowfield most of the party were there before her.

Kitty came rushing in just as the Earl was looking at the clock, with a frown between his eyes.

She was wearing an even more daring gown than she had worn the night before. There was a necklace of emeralds round her neck and emeralds in her hair.

She took the Earl's arm in a possessive manner.

"You are late!" he said uncompromisingly.

"What you should really say is that I'm worth waiting for," Kitty replied.

She had covered herself with a strong, almost overwhelming perfume which Pandora could not help thinking clashed both with the fragrance of the flowers and the smell of lavender and bees'-wax which had always been a part of Chart.

They proceeded into dinner very much as they had the night before, and once again she found herself beside Sir Gilbert.

Last night she had been afraid of him, but tonight she told herself that she had a new confidence and would not allow him to be tiresome.

They were a much smaller party and there were fewer ornaments on the table, but it had been decorated with flowers and Pandora guessed that it was a sign from the gardeners that they too were pleased with the changes.

She felt sure that Michael Farrow would re-employ Mary's father and wondered if perhaps he had

done so already, which would certainly account for
the flowers.

"You are like a flower yourself," Sir Gilbert said
as he followed the direction of her eyes.

"I personally think people are more like animals,"
Pandora retorted, just to be argumentative.

"If that is so, then you are an elusive little fawn
like the ones I have seen in the park," Sir Gilbert said.
"They are alluring little creatures, once you have—
tamed them."

Pandora pretended not to hear what he said, but
she knew it was going to be a difficult dinner, and
she was not mistaken.

Sir Gilbert tried to make love to her and everything she said, however commonplace, he managed
somehow to twist into a compliment.

She realised he was very experienced but she was
sure that any ordinary man would have become
bored or even affronted by her snubbing replies to
such ardent remarks. But not Sir Gilbert!

He continued plaguing her until she was thankful
when the meal came to an end.

"Would you like to take the ladies to the
Salon, Pandora?" the Earl asked.

Pandora rose to her feet, but Kitty cried:

"We're not going to leave you to drink your port
until you're under the table. Either you come with
us or we'll stay with you!"

"Oh, come on, Kitty! Be a sport!" Freddie said.
"We want a glass of port and you are not having any
after what it did to you last night."

"I'm drinking nothing but champagne," Kitty answered, "but I'm staying with Norvin, whatever you
may say."

She glared at Pandora as she added:

"Or whoever else tries to give orders—being in no
position to do so!"

"I will tell Burrows to bring the brandy into the
Salon," the Earl said. "Perhaps Kitty is right and we
should do better without port tonight."

"That has spoilt my evening!" Freddie exclaimed. "But perhaps I will be able to make up for it tomorrow."

"I dare say you will manage to do that," Clive said. "If ever there was a three-bottle man—or should it be a five-bottle man?—that is you, Freddie!"

"Norvin's cellars can stand it," Freddie said quite unabashedly.

They all moved in a body towards the Salon, where to Pandora's surprise she found that there were card-tables laid out.

"We're going to gamble—good!" Hettie exclaimed.

"I hope Clive can afford your losses," Kitty said spitefully. "It cost him a fortune the other night."

"I won quite a bit back the next night," Hettie retorted.

To her relief, Pandora heard Sir Gilbert having a wager with Freddie as to who would draw an ace first.

As she had no wish to gamble and no money to gamble with, she certainly did not want anyone to sponsor her and so she slipped through one of the long windows out onto the terrace.

It was a warm night without a breath of wind and the sky was the beautiful translucent glow of pink that comes just before the dusk.

Pandora thought as she moved down the steps onto the green lawn that there was nowhere in the world that could be as lovely as Chart.

The lake was like a silver mirror reflecting the golden kingcups and the white water-lilies floating on their flat, green leaves.

She could smell the night-scented stock, the roses, and the honeysuckle, which seemed more fragrant than she remembered them.

She walked down to the lake to stand listening to the croak of the frogs and the noise of the crickets.

Overhead she heard the first high note of a bat and she felt that they all spoke to her and she was a part of them.

"Mrs. Meadowfield is right," she told herself. "This

is where I belong, where in fact I have always belonged."

She thought whimsically that wherever she went, even if she never saw Chart Hall or the village again, part of her would remain here, a part of her heart and mind, which she could never forget.

She was so intent on her thoughts that she did not hear anyone approach until a voice she disliked said suavely:

"I have found you, my elusive lady! I had a feeling you might be here."

Sir Gilbert broke the spell and Pandora looked towards him angrily.

"I came out here because I want to be alone," she said.

"And I came because I want to be with you."

"If I am being elusive it is because I have no wish to listen to anything you have to say to me," Pandora answered. "You may think it is rude, but I am telling the truth."

Sir Gilbert laughed.

"I find you different from anyone I have ever known, and it is quite entrancing. You attract me, little Pandora, and I have no intention of leaving you alone."

He moved and Pandora anticipated that he intended to put his arms round her. She tried to escape, but it was too late.

He pulled her against him and she started to struggle desperately, but realised that she was very ineffectual against his strength.

He drew her closer and still closer, and now he bent his head and his lips were seeking hers.

Pandora gave a little cry of alarm because the touch of him revolted her and the idea of his kissing her made her feel disgusted.

Then as she turned her face from side to side Sir Gilbert ceased seeking her mouth and instead picked her up in his arms.

"We will go somewhere a little more secluded," he said. "Then I will teach you not to be defiant."

He spoke in a tone of satisfaction. At the same time, Pandora sensed that she had excited him.

He held her with one arm imprisoned against his chest, and the other was beneath the arm with which he encircled her.

"Put me down!" she cried. "How dare you ... behave like this! I hate you ... do you hear? I hate you!"

"I will teach you to love me," Sir Gilbert replied, "and let me tell you, Pandora, I am a very experienced teacher."

"Let me go! Where are you taking me? Let me go!" Pandora cried again.

She knew he had no intention of doing anything of the sort, and he was carrying her into the bushes at the side of the lake.

The grass was thick there and he put her down on the ground. Then, when she would have scrambled away, he threw himself on top of her.

Now with a scream of terror she pushed both her hands against his chest. But he lifted her chin with his fingers and she knew that nothing she could do would be effective and she was helpless.

She screamed again, and as he looked down at her she saw the fire in his eyes and knew he was savouring the moment when he would silence her cries.

Someone pushed through the shrubs, and the next moment, almost before Pandora could realise what was happening, Sir Gilbert was jerked backwards by a strong hand at the neck of his evening-coat.

Pandora knew it was the Earl, and she felt a relief that was indescribable sweep over her because he was there and because he had saved her.

"What the hell do you think you are doing?" she heard him ask angrily.

He released Sir Gilbert and as he stumbled to his feet the Earl added:

"I thought you were gentleman enough to leave my cousin alone after I spoke to you last night."

"Why should I leave her alone?" Sir Gilbert asked furiously. "You have your fun and I want mine."

"Not with my cousin!"

"I will not be ordered about by you!" Sir Gilbert retorted.

Without any warning he hit out at the Earl, and would have smashed into the side of his face if the Earl had not seen the blow coming and moved with a fraction of a second to spare.

However, the blow caught him on his shoulder and he staggered.

Then his fists were up and he struck back at Sir Gilbert in a manner which told Pandora that he was an experienced pugilist.

Sir Gilbert, however, was experienced too, and in a moment they had moved out from the shelter of the shrubs and onto the lawn.

They fought furiously, but managed to parry each other's blows, until suddenly, unexpectedly, the Earl broke through Sir Gilbert's guard and caught him on the point of the chin.

The older man staggered backwards, and as they were now fighting on the edge of the lake, he slipped on the reeds which bordered it and slowly tipped into the water.

Only as Pandora and the Earl stood watching him, almost fascinated, did the sound of clapping make them both turn in surprise to find that Freddie, Clive, and Richard had been watching them.

"Damned good, Norvin!" Freddie ejaculated. "I had no idea you could be so pugnacious!"

"I learnt in a hard school," the Earl replied briefly.

He walked forward as he spoke and pulled Sir Gilbert out of the water.

He was for the moment unconscious, but now as he shook his head and started spluttering and spitting, the other men ran forward to give him a hand and get him to his feet.

"It was a cursed good fight!" Clive exclaimed.

"And now that you have both got it out of your system, I think we all need a drink."

The Earl held out his hand.

"No hard feelings, Gilbert, and I assure you, I did not mean you to drown."

Sir Gilbert pushed back his hair from his forehead, but he ignored the Earl's hand. He merely looked at him with an expression in his eyes that was one of hatred.

"I demand satisfaction from you, Chartwood!" he said. "And, by God, I intend to have it!"

There was silence after he had spoken. Then Freddie said:

"Oh, come on, Gilbert, be a sport. It was a fair fight and there is no doubt that Norvin won."

"We will fight again tomorrow morning," Sir Gilbert said.

"Are you really proposing a duel?" the Earl enquired. "God Almighty, Gilbert, the whole affair is over. I am quite prepared to say I am sorry I was so rough with you."

"Are you too cowardly to behave like a gentleman?" Sir Gilbert asked aggressively.

"I do not intend to be called a coward!" the Earl retorted.

"Very well, six o'clock tomorrow," Sir Gilbert said. "Clive, I ask you to be one of my seconds, and as I do not intend to sleep in this house tonight, Trentham will provide me with another."

"You cannot be serious!" Freddie protested.

With a dignity which was somehow commendable considering that he was both wet and humiliated, Sir Gilbert walked back alone towards the house.

They stood in silence and watched him go, until Freddie exclaimed:

"I'll be damned. I had no idea he was that sort!"

For the first time Pandora spoke.

"You must not . . . fight a duel," she said to the Earl. "It is . . . very wrong and it might be . . . dangerous."

"It will be dangerous if Gilbert has anything to do with it," Clive said. "He has a nasty reputation for picking duels with inexperienced young men."

"Well, I am not inexperienced," the Earl said sharply. "Freddie and Richard—you will act for me."

"I have no wish to be Gilbert's second," Clive said.

"You have no choice," the Earl answered. "We will meet at six o'clock. I suppose it had better be in the park. We do not want the gardeners as spectators."

"Can nobody . . . stop this?" Pandora pleaded pathetically.

Nobody answered her for a moment. Then as if Clive understood what she was feeling he said quietly:

"It is an affair of honour. I should not say anything to the other women. They will only make a fuss."

"No . . . of course . . . not," Pandora agreed.

She looked at the Earl and wanted to tell him how grateful she was to him for saving her. At the same time, she had never envisaged that anything like this would happen.

She could hardly believe that he was to fight a duel because of her.

"I am sorry! I am sorry!" she wanted to tell him, but he was walking away in a manner which told them all that he wished to be alone.

He did not go back to the house but disappeared into the garden.

Forlornly and in silence Pandora and the men walked back towards the lighted windows of the house.

Chapter Five

As soon as Pandora and the three men entered the Salon from the terrace, Kitty cried out in a furious voice:

"Where the hell've you all been? And where's Norvin? I told you to bring him back with you."

"We could not find him," Freddie answered, "but I expect he will turn up in a moment or two."

"There's something funny going on here," Kitty said disagreeably, "and I don't like it!"

Pandora did not wait to hear any more. She walked across the Salon and without speaking to anyone went into the hall and closed the door behind her.

She realised that once again the three women had had too much to drink, and Caro was in fact sprawling across a sofa with her eyes closed.

'How can gentlemen find them amusing when they look like that?' she wondered.

She had noticed at dinner how much they drank and how each glass seemed to make them noisier and more vulgar in their behavior.

She could not help wondering what old Burrows thought, but he was too well trained to look anything but impassive.

She saw him rebuke with a steely glance one of the footmen who sniggered at something which had been said.

"If only Chart Hall could be like it used to be," she said with a sigh.

Then everything was swept from her mind but the thought that in the morning the Earl would be fighting a duel on her account.

She was sure that he would be a match for Sir Gilbert. At the same time, duels could be dangerous, and she remembered stories she had read or heard of tragedies occurring when men were fighting each other and how the victor often had to flee the country for fear of being arrested.

She was certain nothing like that would happen here. But still she was afraid.

It was her fault, and yet what could she have done except not to have been so foolish as to go out alone in the garden?

She might have guessed, she thought now, that Sir Gilbert would follow her even though she thought he would have been too concerned with his gaming.

"It will be all right . . . I am sure it will be . . . all right," she tried to promise herself optimistically, but all the same she felt afraid.

Mary came to help her undress, but for once she was not interested in anything the girl had to tell her. When she was alone Pandora got into bed, but only to lie sleepless in the darkness.

She began to pray frantically that everything would be all right and the Earl would not be hurt.

If he was even scratched in such an encounter, he might be angry with her and blame her for the whole occurrence.

The idea was so distressing that sleep seemed to retreat even further from her.

About an hour and a half later Pandora heard the rest of the party coming upstairs to bed and they were certainly very noisy about it.

She thought that if they were as drunk as they sounded, they might damage the beautiful State-Rooms in which they were sleeping.

She thought that the Earl had deliberately chosen such accommodation for his guests because he wanted to shock the Chart ancestors, who doubtless would have felt as contemptuous as she did at the drunkenness of the actresses.

She was also surprised and shocked at a great deal of what they said and did.

She could not help watching wide-eyed when at dinner Caro had kissed Richard passionately.

Hettie had put one arm round Freddie's neck and her other hand inside his shirt when she was pleading with him to give her a piece of jewellery she had seen in Bond Street.

Pandora kept wondering what her mother would have thought or said in the circumstances.

Then once again she told herself she had no right to criticise. She had invited herself here, and if the Earl's guests behaved outrageously, she had been warned that that was what she would find.

At the same time, she resented everything they did, because it proved that Prosper Witheridge was right and the gossiping old women of Lindchester had every justification for feeling outraged.

'I am sure Norvin will begin to see how terrible they are,' she thought.

Then she told herself that in the beauty and dignity of Chart Hall no-one could fail to notice the contrast.

There was no need for her to say anything, even if she had the opportunity. Chart itself would point the lesson.

She was sure that the Earl was quite sensitive enough to perceive the contrast between Caro lying drunkenly on the sofa and above her the portrait of the Countess of Chartwood, painted exquisitely by Sir Joshua Reynolds.

She looked so lovely and graceful yet at the same time so dignified and well bred that one's eyes were held by the picture.

"He must see, he must," Pandora whispered to herself, and added some words she remembered from *Paradise Lost*:

Abash'd the Devil stood,
And felt how awful goodness is, and saw
Virtue in her shape how lovely.

"He will see ... I know he will see sooner or later," Pandora consoled herself, but still she could not sleep.

She heard the clock over the stables strike two, then the half hour.

Everything was very still and because she felt wide awake with the thoughts pursuing each other in her mind, she rose to walk to one of the windows.

She pulled back the silk curtains and stood looking out at the beauty beneath her.

The stars were brilliant and there was a half-moon high over the great trees in the park.

She thought of what would take place in the morning and once again she was praying that the Earl would not be hurt.

"He must not lose all this now," she whispered to herself.

The moonlight was shining on the West Wing, which was nearest to her, while the East was still in shadow.

It glinted silver on the long windows that Inigo Jones had designed so symmetrically. Then, as she looked, Pandora saw that a window on the ground floor was open.

'The servants must have forgotten,' she thought.

She remembered how insistent her grandfather had always been that the lower windows of the house should be securely fastened at night.

"It would be easy for anyone to climb in by them," he had said often enough, "and it is doubtful if the nightwatchmen would hear them."

There had always been two nightwatchmen at Chart Hall, Underwood and Colby by name, unless they had been sacked. They were both elderly men and their hearing was not as good as it might have been.

'I will find one of them,' Pandora decided, 'and tell him about the window.'

By the light of the moon she put on her dressing-gown, a pale blue silk which had belonged to her mother and which was trimmed with lace down the front and on the wide sleeves.

Pandora buttoned it and tied the sash tightly round her small waist. She slipped her feet into the blue slippers which matched the dressing-gown.

She opened the door of her room and went out into the corridor.

Most of the candles in the sconces had been extinguished, but there were enough left for her to see her way, even though she would have been able to find it blindfolded.

She thought Underwood or Colby would be in the hall, which was where they usually ended up their rounds, but there was nobody there.

After looking vainly along the corridor which led to the Library, Pandora walked in the opposite direction, past the rooms which lay between the Salon and the Dining-Room.

There was no sign of either of the men. She guessed she would find them in the kitchen-quarters, drinking a glass of ale or having something to eat.

'They are certainly more slack than they were in Grandpapa's time,' she thought.

She passed through the green-baize door which cut off the main part of the house from the kitchen, scullery-larder, still-room, servants'-hall, and the other offices.

Before she reached them Pandora had to pass the pantry.

She suddenly remembered that if she could not find the nightwatchmen there was always a footman sleeping in the pantry to guard the safe where the silver was kept.

She had often thought as a child that he could not be very comfortable, because he had a bed which shut up against the wall in the daytime and was pulled down only at night.

She had almost reached the pantry, moving silently in her soft slippers, when she heard voices.

'So this is where the nightwatchmen are,' she thought, smiling, 'gossipping!'

She took a few more steps; then, seeing something lying at the side of the passage, she looked down, wondering what it was.

It was not easy to see clearly. Then with a shock of surprise she saw that it was Underwood who was lying stretched out on the floor.

For a moment she thought he was asleep, but then another, more frightening thought occurred to her.

Without realising what she was doing, she ran into the pantry for help, then stood in the doorway, transfixed with horror.

Gagged and trussed up against one wall was the footman, the safe door was open, and standing in front of it with a gold ornament in his hand was Dalton.

Another man, who she was sure from the description she had heard of him was Mr. Anstey, was holding a sack open.

She gave a gasp of sheer horror, and Dalton, who had his back to her, turned. As he did so, Mr. Anstey asked:

"Who's this?"

"His Lordship's cousin," Dalton replied, "and I suspect it was her interference that got me dismissed!"

As he spoke he moved towards Pandora and too late she realised the danger she was in.

She tried to run away, but he was too quick for her and in a moment had caught her arms behind her back and was tying her wrists.

"Let me go! How dare you!" Pandora began to say; then she screamed.

The sound had hardly left her lips before Mr. Anstey gagged her. She tried to struggle but it was impossible.

Then, when she thought despairingly that she was completely in their power, a voice from the doorway asked furiously:

"What is going on here?"

Pandora's heart gave a leap of relief, for it was the Earl and she saw that in his hand he held a duelling-pistol.

"Release that lady immediately," he commanded, "or I will shoot you where you stand!"

He had his pistol pointed at Dalton, but Mr. Anstey put his arm round Pandora and holding her against him pulled her back against the door of the safe.

"Not so fast!" he said to the Earl.

Now with a feeling of horror Pandora realised that he had a sharp knife at her throat.

"You may kill Dalton, M'Lord," he said, "but your cousin'll be dead too. Then if you wish we can fight it out man-to-man."

Pandora wanted to give a cry of sheer horror, but she knew that the duelling-pistol held only one bullet, and the point of the knife was sharp against her throat.

Mr. Anstey had command of the situation.

"Pick up the sacks," he said to Dalton. "And now, M'Lord, you'll let us pass or you'll find that I'm not speaking idly when I tell you that this pretty young lady'll be lying dead at your feet."

There was something evil in the way he mouthed the words, as if they gave him satisfaction.

"You will not get away with this," the Earl said.

"I think you'll find I'm better and more experienced at being a thief than you are at being a nobleman," Mr. Anstey retorted.

Pandora saw the anger in the Earl's eyes and she thought for a moment he might risk the consequences and shoot either Mr. Anstey or Dalton.

If she died it would be for a worthy cause, for she could not bear to think of these unscrupulous men taking away the historic gold and silver ornaments that had belonged to her ancestors.

"Go ahead!" Mr. Anstey said to Dalton. "His Lordship is powerless, and won't hurt you, as he well knows."

With his knife still at Pandora's throat and holding her so hard against his chest that it was painful, he moved slowly forward, his eyes on the Earl.

"People die very quick when their jugular vein's been severed," he said evilly. "Just a slip of the hand, M'Lord, and her blood'll flow!"

Slowly, as if every step was agony to him, the Earl backed out of the doorway.

Pandora could read his thoughts in that she knew he was wondering if he dared fire at Mr. Anstey's head.

She wanted to cry out to him to take the risk and if she was killed too it would not matter, but she was propelled forward by the man who was using her as a shield.

Then they were backing away down the flagged passage which led past the kitchen and the Earl could only stand and watch them go.

As they reached the door that led to the kitchen-yard Pandora saw him turn and run back the way he had come, and she was quite certain that he was on his way to the stables to get help.

The moment he disappeared, the man who was holding her was galvanised into action.

He took his arm from round her and dragged her out into the kitchen-yard and across it to where outside the tradesmen's entrance there stood a cart.

Dalton was already there and was dumping the sacks into it. It was a light vehicle drawn by two horses and Pandora knew it could move very fast.

She hardly had time, however, to think of anything besides her own discomfort, for Mr. Anstey picked her up in his arms and flung her on top of the sacks.

Then with a swiftness she would not have believed possible, he and Dalton climbed up onto the high seats in front of the cart and the horses were away.

The cart was very light and the horses moved so quickly that Pandora knew they would be out of the drive and onto the main road long before the Earl would be able to awaken the grooms and have horses saddled with which to follow them.

The rough way she had been thrown on top of the sacks was extremely painful.

As the horses galloped through the lodge gates she was not only propelled from side to side, but the cart rattled in a manner which made her think she would not only be bruised all over but might easily have bones broken.

"We'll get away," she heard Dalton say above the noise of the wheels. "We've got a good start."

"What was he doing walking about at this time of night with a pistol in his hand?" Mr. Anstey asked.

"No idea," Dalton replied.

They had to shout at each other above the noise of the horses' hoofs, the wheels, and the clatter of their loot.

Pushing against the sides of the cart with her feet, Pandora managed to slip off the sacks and lie beside them instead of on top of them.

That made her more comfortable, but the gag was still biting into her cheeks, and as her hands were tied behind her back it was impossible to prevent her arms from being bruised with every movement.

'Oh, God, please let Norvin catch us and save me,' Pandora prayed.

She had the sudden idea that when they ceased fleeing to avoid capture, these men would not trouble to take her any further.

They would kill her and throw her into a ditch. They would have no wish to leave her alive, and as they would hang anyway for robbery, the penalty could not be increased for murder.

'Help me, oh . . . please . . . help me!' she cried in her heart, and wondered if her father knew what was happening to her and if he could somehow assist the Earl to save her.

There was no-one else who could do so, for only

the Earl knew what had happened and he alone
would be aware of the danger she was in.

Pandora tried to calculate how long it would
take the Earl to follow them. Then she heard Mr.
Anstey, who was driving, shout:

"Look back, and if he's following us, shoot him!
You'll find a pistol in my left-hand pocket."

"Then why the hell didn't you use it before?"
Dalton asked in an angry tone.

"He took me by surprise," Mr. Anstey admitted,
"and anyway the knife was handy, so what are you
complaining about?"

"Nothing," Dalton replied, "but I'd like him
dead."

"Then shoot if there's a sight or a sign of him,"
Mr. Anstey commanded.

Now Dalton turned round in his seat, looking
backwards along the road on which they had come,
and Pandora felt she must scream in sheer terror.

She was quite certain that it would never occur
to the Earl that the thieves had a pistol, since they
had not used it in Chart Hall.

He would merely come riding after them and
would be shot down, and she too would die.

There was nothing she could do but pray—pray
desperately with her whole heart and soul. Then,
almost to her surprise, she found herself thinking:

'If I have to die it would not matter much...
but let the Earl live...I think now he has begun to
like Chart and he will...keep and preserve it as it
...should be.'

She prayed with such intensity that she shut her
eyes.

Then suddenly there was a noise like an explo-
sion, the whole world seemed to turn a somersault,
there were cries and turmoil, shouts, and the frightened neighing of the horses.

Whatever had happened had banged her head
and Pandora saw stars whirling round her...for a
few seconds she must have been unconscious....

It was almost surprising to find that she was

still alive and somebody was lifting her out of the cart and holding her closely in his arms.

"Norvin!" she wanted to exclaim, but she was still gagged.

She felt his fingers undoing the knot while he supported her head against his shoulder.

Then she gave a deep gasp which turned into a sound of fear.

"It is all right," he said. "You are not really hurt. I took a chance on my belief that they would put you at the back with what they had stolen."

She found it impossible to understand what he was saying.

Then, supporting her with one hand, he started to undo the rope which held her hands together, and as she looked she saw incredible confusion on the road.

The horses were down on their knees, the cart with one wheel off was lying at a strange angle, and in the roadway where obviously they had been thrown from the high seat of the cart were two bodies.

Pandora stared, not understanding what had happened. Then the Earl explained as he finished untying her:

"It was hard on the horses, poor beasts, but a rope across the road which tripped them was safer than risking a firing match when you were in the power of those fiends."

"A . . . rope across the . . . road?" Pandora murmured.

"The trees made it easy," he said and she thought he smiled with satisfaction.

"How did you . . . reach us so . . . quickly?"

"The grooms knew a way across the fields," he answered. "Another time I shall know it myself."

His arms still were round her and she was leaning against him.

"You . . . saved me!" she murmured. "I . . . prayed that you would . . . do so."

"I guessed that that was what you would be doing," the Earl remarked, "and of course the prayers of Saints are always heard!"

She tried to laugh because she knew that he wanted her to do so, but instead she felt very near to tears.

It had all been so frightening, but she might have guessed, she thought, that because he was a Chart he would find a way out of any situation, however difficult.

The grooms were tying up Mr. Anstey and Dalton, who were still unconscious.

They trussed them like chickens. Then one of the men whom Pandora remembered came up to the Earl to ask:

"What do you want done with them, M'Lord?"

"Leave them at the side of the road," the Earl answered. "We will send later and have them taken before the Magistrates. And turn the horses loose."

"Very good, M'Lord."

"I suppose you will be able to manage the sacks between you?"

"We'll see to them, M'Lord," the groom answered and grinned.

He glanced at Pandora as if he asked a question, and the Earl said:

"I will take Miss Stratton back on my saddle."

Another groom brought the Earl's horse from where it must have been concealed in the trees.

He took his arms from Pandora gently, as if he was afraid she would not be able to stand on her own. When he found that she could do so, he pulled off his evening-coat and laid it on the front of the saddle.

"I will mount first," he said to the groom, "then hand Miss Stratton up to me."

"Very good, M'Lord."

The Earl swung himself up on the saddle. Then, reaching down while the groom lifted her, he pulled Pandora up in front of him so that she was sitting sideways and his left arm held her securely.

"We will take it easy," he said, "now that there is no need to hurry."

Because she could not help herself Pandora

turned her face against his shoulder so that he could not see her tears.

"I . . . th-thought they would . . . k-kill me," she whispered.

"It is all over," the Earl said quietly. "And surely you must remember this is an adventure that I shall be able to relate to my grandsons, or was it my great-grandsons with whom I had to concern myself?"

Pandora gave a choking little laugh.

"It was . . . my fault. I might have guessed when I saw the . . . open window that it would be Dalton who was trying to . . . rob you."

"It would have been wiser to have informed me rather than try to take them on single-handedly!" the Earl said.

They were moving slowly towards home as Pandora replied:

"Actually, I was looking for the nightwatchmen. But they had knocked Underwood insensible."

"I told one of the grooms before I left to see to him and to the wretched footman."

"You thought of everything!" Pandora said admiringly.

"For an amateur at this sort of adventure, you must admit I did not do too badly!" the Earl said. "You certainly create an unprecedented amount of drama and excitement. I had always imagined the country was a quiet place with nothing to do!"

Pandora thought he was also referring to the duel, and after a moment she said in a very small voice:

"Must you . . . fight . . . him?"

"It will give me intense pleasure to do so," the Earl replied. "The man is a swine and deserves all he gets."

"But he is . . . dangerous. He has fought a great many . . . duels."

"So have I, in one way or another," the Earl replied, "and I will try not to disgrace the family name in this instance, whatever I may do in others."

"I could not bear . . ." Pandora began.

There was a pause.

"Bear what?" the Earl asked.

"For you to be . . . hurt on my . . . account. It was so . . . foolish of me to go into the garden . . . alone."

"Extremely foolish when there is that sort of cad about," the Earl agreed, "but how were you to know?"

"In a way it was even more . . . frightening than thinking I might be . . . killed!"

She was speaking to herself more than to the Earl. Then she felt his arm tighten round her.

"They are neither of them experiences that should ever have happened to you," he said.

She was suddenly conscious of being close to him. He was wearing only a white lawn shirt, and she could feel the warmth of his body against her cheek and the strength of his arm that held her.

She was acutely aware of him as a man.

She had never been as close as this to any other man or indeed known such a feeling of security and safety.

They rode on in silence until unexpectedly the Earl remarked:

"Your hair smells of violets."

"I wash it with a herbal lotion which Mama used to make," Pandora replied. "There are masses of violets in the spring in the garden at the Vicarage, and she would distil a scent from them."

As she spoke she thought of the strong, exotic perfume that Kitty used, and she wondered if that was what the Earl preferred.

He did not say any more, and now Pandora realised that they had left the road and were moving through the fields which bordered the park.

"We are nearly home," she said, "and the gold and silver is safe. If in the morning we had awakened to find it gone, I would have cried my eyes out."

The Earl did not speak and after a moment she said a little hesitatingly:

"You . . . would have . . . minded?"

She saw his lips twist in a smile. Then he said:

"I know what you want me to say, and ordinarily

I would be damned if I would have you bullying me! But because you have been through a harrowing experience I will spoil you and say: Yes, I would have minded!"

Pandora gave a little sigh.

"I thought you . . . would."

"If there is one thing I really dislike," the Earl said, "it is women who say: 'I told you so!' "

He was, however, not speaking aggressively.

"I am not saying anything," Pandora replied. "I just want you to . . . love Chart."

As she spoke she realised that they could see the Castle in the valley below them.

It was breathtakingly beautiful in the moonlight, which seemed to turn the great building to silver. She gave a little exclamation.

"It is yours . . . all yours!"

She felt the Earl's arm tighten as if it were an instinctive response which he could not help, and because it seemed to draw her closer to him even than she was already, she felt again a strange, unaccountable feeling run through her.

It was a feeling she had never known before, and yet it was so ecstatic, so lovely, that it was like the moonlight itself.

Then the Earl urged his horse forward and they were moving quickly towards Chart Hall.

*   *   *

In her bed-room Pandora felt as if she had lived through a long and strange dream.

It hardly seemed possible that she had been through so much in the short time since she had left her bed and gone to the window to look out at the moonlight.

The Earl had wanted her to have a drink when they arrived back, but she had refused.

"Then go to bed," he said. "You must be tired after all you have been through."

"You must go to bed too," she replied quickly.

"I am used to going without sleep," he answered.

At the same time, as they stood in the hall he seemed hardly to be thinking of what he should say, but was looking at her with a strange expression in his eyes.

Old Burrows had the door open and was waiting for them. He had been aroused by the groom who had gone back to release the trussed-up footman.

"There are drinks and something to eat, M'Lord, in the Morning-Room," Burrows said in his quiet, unobtrusive manner.

"Thank you," the Earl said. "Is the nightwatchman all right?"

"They knocked him unconscious, M'Lord, but apart from a bad headache there are no bones broken."

"Well, that is a relief," the Earl exclaimed.

Pandora had already climbed three steps of the Great Staircase when she stopped with her hand on the bannister to listen to Burrows's reply.

The Earl walked to the foot of the stairs to stand looking up at her.

"I suppose I ought to thank you," he said. "If you had not interfered and put your life in danger, they might not only have taken the gold and silver ornaments but a great many other things as well."

"If you start thanking me, I shall have to thank you again for rescuing me."

"Then I will just say go to bed and forget it," the Earl smiled, "and remember, it is not a thing that is likely to happen a second time."

"I hope not," Pandora replied.

Then she remembered the duel which still lay ahead.

"You will be very careful . . . promise me!"

She saw in his eyes that he understood to what she was referring, and he replied cynically:

"I wonder how many people would be delighted if Sir Gilbert shoots me down."

Pandora gave a little cry.

"Do not speak . . . like that . . . it is . . . unlucky."

"I have told you—I am not afraid of him."

"You should never ... underestimate the enemy."

"No, you are right! And, as you have asked me— I will take care."

"Please ... please do ... that!"

Pandora's eyes met his and for a moment it seemed as if both of them were very still.

Then because she felt shy, because she was suddenly conscious that she was wearing only her dressing-gown and her hair was falling over her shoulders, she turned and ran up the stairs.

❋   ❋   ❋

In bed, Pandora surprisingly fell asleep almost as soon as her head touched the pillow.

She expected that if she was not kept awake by the horror of what had happened she would be unable to sleep because her body was aching from the bruises she had sustained in the cart.

It must have been because she had been so battered that when she turned over she awoke with a start, and knew it was a pain in her arm which had aroused her.

"Mrs. Meadowfield will have some embrocation to put on it," she told herself.

She moved her legs and found that they too were painful.

The ornaments in the sack had dug sharply into them and she thought perhaps the skin had been broken.

Then suddenly her thoughts startled her into an awareness that she had been asleep, that it was morning, and that the Earl was fighting a duel.

She sat up in bed and realised that there was light on either side of the curtains.

"It is dawn!" she told herself.

She got out of bed, feeling as if her body ached all over, and pulled back one of the curtains.

The first rays of the sun were showing golden in the East. The sky was still purple overhead but the stars were fading.

'It must be five o'clock,' she thought, but when she peered at the clock on the mantelshelf she found it was after half-past.

She looked out the window. There was no-one about.

She was aware that women never attended duels, but she told herself that this was an exceptional case because she was involved.

'I will not let anyone see me,' she thought, 'but I must watch what happens.'

She dressed quickly, then thought that it would be more difficult for anyone to notice her in her light summer gown if she wore over it the green cape in which she had arrived at Chart Hall.

Now she was ready and she went again to the window to wait.

About ten minutes later she saw the Earl, accompanied by Freddie and Richard, come out from a side door which was situated beyond the Library.

She knew they had not used the front door so that the footman who was on duty would not be aware that they had left the house.

They walked across the court-yard beneath Pandora's window and she thought how elegant they all looked.

The Earl, who was walking between the other two men, seemed in her eyes outstanding, a man, she felt, who would be noticed wherever he might be.

'It is because he is a Chart,' she thought triumphantly, and she felt he would laugh at her if he knew what she was thinking.

Then as they reached the bridge she saw a Phaeton coming down the drive and realised that Sir Gilbert was arriving.

She felt a sudden agony of apprehension in her breast which swept away the thoughts of everything else.

A duel was to be fought because of her, and now she was afraid with a terror which seemed to strike through her as if it were forked lightning.

She ran from her room and down the stairs to let herself out through a different door from the one the Earl had used, one that did not involve her passing through the Hall.

She realised that the duellists were making for a glade that stood on the left side of the bridge, which, she had been told, had in ancient days been used as a bowling-green.

It had now lapsed into disuse, but the gardeners automatically cut the grass because they always had done so.

Surrounded by shrubs, it was concealed and could not be overlooked and was in fact an excellent site for a duel.

There was no chance of those from the house who had gone ahead, or of Sir Gilbert, who had followed them, seeing Pandora cross the bridge. Knowing the way, she kept to the shadows of the bushes until she heard voices.

Then, moving very, very cautiously, she approached through the shrubs until she had a sight of the seconds standing in the centre of the bowling-green and beside them a man she recognised as Sir Edward Trentham and another man.

She guessed that Sir Gilbert had brought a friend with him as a referee.

There was no doubt that that was his office, for as soon as Pandora was within ear-shot she heard him intoning:

"Five—six—seven—"

She could see now, by moving the leaves a little, that the Earl was walking away to her right and Sir Gilbert to the left.

"Eight—nine—ten!"

The two men turned and fired simultaneously. It was impossible to be certain which pistol fired first.

For a moment Pandora felt everything swim dizzily before her eyes and it was difficult to see what had happened.

Then she saw the Earl put his hand up to his head and as he did so he fell to the ground.

She gave a little cry and burst through the bushes, and as she ran towards him, Freddie was beside her.

The Earl was lying on the ground and she could see blood pouring down the side of his face from his temple.

For one terrifying second, Pandora thought that he was dead.

"He has only been grazed," Freddie said in tones of satisfaction.

Then as the horror of it swept over her she thought she knew that she loved him.

It was all an incredible muddle, her love, her feeling of terror, and her relief in one part of her mind as she understood what Freddie had said.

Then as she slipped her arm under the Earl's head and lifted him against her, Richard came running up to say:

"He got Gilbert in the arm. We should have thought of having a Doctor here."

"We must get Norvin back to the house," Pandora said.

"Yes, of course," Freddie agreed. "Shall we carry him?"

Pandora looked down at the Earl's closed eyes.

"I think it would be better if we put him on a gate."

She remembered it was what her father always did when there were casualties in the hunting-field.

"Yes, of course," Richard agreed. "But where will we find one?"

Pandora thought quickly.

"Beyond the shrubs there," she said, pointing to the far end of the bowling-green. "There is a gate into an orchard."

Freddie and Richard ran off without her saying any more, and now she tried to stanch with her handkerchief the blood that was still running down the Earl's cheeks.

It made a crimson stain on his shirt and she was

suddenly afraid, with a fear which seemed to pierce her, that he was mortally wounded.

A bullet in the arm could easily be extracted, but an injury to the head could be very serious indeed, for she was well aware that the Doctors knew little or nothing about injuries to the brain.

Then she told herself reassuringly as she wiped away the blood that the bullet was not lodged in the Earl's head but must have swept along the side of his temple, searing its way through his hair.

'Sir Gilbert aimed deliberately at his head,' she thought.

As an experienced shot, it would have been impossible for him to have missed the Earl's left arm, which had been turned towards him, or for the bullet to have passed so high unless he had aimed it so.

Even as she thought of it she looked up to find Sir Gilbert walking unsteadily towards her, his uninjured arm round the shoulders of Sir Edward Trentham.

His wounded arm was tied roughly with a handkerchief through which the blood was already spreading in a crimson tide.

"Norvin is all right, I hope?" he asked as he reached Pandora.

She looked up at him with furious eyes.

"You tried to kill him!" she said accusingly. "You are too good a shot to have hit him in the head unless you intended to do so."

She saw by the expression in Sir Gilbert's eyes that what she had said was true.

"Now that is a ridiculous suggestion . . ." he began, but Sir Edward interrupted, saying:

"It is certainly unlike you, Gilbert, to be so far off the mark."

"Pandora is right," Clive exclaimed, who had been listening, "and by God, if Norvin dies I will see that you swing for it!"

"You are all hysterical," Sir Gilbert said sourly.

"Take me home, Edward. I have no wish to listen to such absurd accusations."

"Are they so absurd?" Sir Edward questioned as he helped Sir Gilbert walk away.

"Damn him!" Clive exclaimed. "I have always heard that he is a killer, and it is true."

He dropped down on his knees beside the Earl and asked:

"He is not really bad, is he?"

"I hope . . . not," Pandora answered, but her voice was uncertain.

She went on holding the Earl and tried to mop away the blood, accepting Clive's handkerchief as hers was already saturated.

Freddie and Richard came back with the gate.

Very gently they lifted the Earl onto it, then all three men started to carry him back to the house.

Pandora started to run ahead of them.

"Take him to the front door," she said. "It will be easier to get him up the Great Staircase, and I will go ahead and see that his room is ready and send a groom for the Doctor."

She ran as swiftly as she could, to find the front door already open and two maids in mob-caps scrubbing the steps.

To her relief, Mrs. Meadowfield was in the Hall.

"His Lordship has been injured," Pandora said breathlessly.

"Mr. Burrows was certain something strange was going on," Mrs. Meadowfield exclaimed. "What's happened to His Lordship?"

"He has been shot in the head in a duel," Pandora explained. "Send a groom immediately for Dr. Graham."

"Yes, of course, Miss!" Mrs. Meadowfield cried. "He'll know what to do."

It certainly was a relief, Pandora thought, when half an hour later the Doctor arrived.

She had not changed since they had brought the Earl back to the house, and her cotton gown was marked with blood, but she had no intention of doing anything about it until she heard what the Doctor had to say.

It seemed to her as if a century passed while she waited, but all the time she was aware of how much the Earl meant to her in a way that she had never envisaged for one moment she could feel for him.

She thought now it was inevitable, seeing he was so different from the other men she had known.

Yet he was also part of her blood and part of everything she had ever cared for, so it was natural that she should fall in love with him like any infatuated school-girl.

"I am a fool!" she told herself. "He has Kitty, and all those other fascinating women to give him the gaiety and the amusement that he really enjoys. It is impossible that he should look at anyone like me."

Now as she stood outside in the corridor, the mere idea of Kitty sleeping next door to the Earl in the bed-room that had been her grandmother's hurt her in a way that she knew was jealousy.

"How can I be so absurd? So idiotic?" she questioned. "Tomorrow I have to go back to Lindchester and perhaps I will never see him again, nor will he want to see me."

The idea was an agony in itself, then she told herself that her feelings were quite unimportant so long as he got well and was not permanently injured in any way by Sir Gilbert's treachery.

Dr. Graham came from the Earl's room and Pandora ran towards him.

"What do you . . . think? Has he been hurt . . . seriously? Will he . . . get well?"

The questions tumbled out of her lips one after the other and Dr. Graham put his arm round her shoulders.

"Now, Pandora, this is very unlike you," he said. "You are always so brave and sensible."

"Yes, I know," Pandora said, "but this . . ."

"Is unpleasant, of course," the Doctor finished,

"but I think with careful nursing there will be no complications and we will soon have His Lordship back on his feet."

"Do you mean that?" Pandora asked breathlessly.

"You have always trusted me in the past," Dr. Graham replied.

"And I trust you now," Pandora said, "and I am so very glad you are here."

"His Lordship will want careful nursing for the next forty-eight hours or so," the Doctor said. "He may run a high temperature, and he will most likely be delirious. He just needs to be watched so that he does nothing stupid, and I will be back again in an hour or so."

"I will nurse him," Pandora said quickly.

"I thought you would say that," the Doctor said with a smile. "Well, I have seen you being very efficient in the sick-room when your father was laid up after a hunting accident, and you and your mother have done more than anyone else for the people of the village."

"You must tell me what I am to do," Pandora said.

"I have told Mrs. Meadowfield," the Doctor replied. "You can take it turn and turn about to sit with him, and his valet seems to be a sensible chap as well."

Pandora was silent for a moment. Then she said:

"Do you think the . . . wound will in any way . . . affect his . . . brain?"

"That is such an unlikely contingency that I think there is no reason to worry about it," the Doctor replied.

He paused, then added:

"Whoever shot His Lordship was either inexperienced or else was doing his best to commit murder."

"That is what I think too," Pandora said.

"Why must these young men risk their lives?" Dr. Graham asked.

Then he smiled.

"I suppose," he continued, "it is an honourable way of deciding an argument, but as far as the professional man is concerned, I often think it is a pity we have progressed further than bows and arrows."

Pandora tried to laugh.

She was used to the Doctor's rather droll sayings.

They reached the top of the staircase and he patted Pandora on the shoulder.

"Now you go and change your dress and have a rest," he said. "You can leave the Earl safely in Mrs. Meadowfield's hands for the next few hours."

He glanced at the grandfather-clock ticking in the Hall below them.

"I will be back about noon," he said, "but I expect him still to look very much as he does now, so do not get upset about it."

"I will try not to," Pandora said.

The Doctor smiled at her.

"That sounds more like your mother's daughter," he said, and walked down the stairs.

Pandora sped back to the Earl's bed-room.

She entered it quietly to find Mrs. Meadowfield tidying the room.

The Doctor had bandaged the Earl's head, and he was lying still on his back with his eyes closed and appeared very much as he had before, except that he was paler.

Pandora looked at him with a prayer in her heart that the Doctor was right and there was no real damage.

'I love you!' she said to him silently. 'I love you and you must hurry and get well because there are so many things that need your attention.'

Chapter Six

Pandora changed her gown, but she did not rest as the Doctor had suggested. Instead, she went downstairs to the Dining-Room where she knew the gentlemen would be having breakfast.

They rose as she entered and Burrows hurried forward to offer her a number of dishes. Although she was not hungry she accepted a little to eat and waited until the servants had left the room.

"What did the Doctor say?" Freddie asked as if he could bear the suspense no longer.

"He said," Pandora answered, choosing her words carefully, "that Norvin must be carefully nursed and have complete . . . quiet for the next . . . few days."

She looked directly at Freddie as she spoke and he understood at once what she had left unsaid.

"We will leave before luncheon."

"What you really mean is, as soon as we can get the women out of bed and packed up," Richard remarked.

Again Freddie met Pandora's eyes and after a moment he said, turning to Richard:

"Who is going to take Kitty?"

"Will she leave?" Richard enquired.

"It is time she went back to London anyway for rehearsals," Freddie said. "She will not want to lose her part in *The Beggar's Opera*."

"Then you persuade her," Richard said dryly.

"Is Ellison putting on that old show again?" Clive enquired.

"It is always a success," Freddie replied, "and with Madame Vestris as Captain Macheath in breeches, how could it fail?"

Pandora was listening and she thought it extraordinary that any woman should be prepared to appear in public wearing men's attire.

She wondered what Prosper Witheridge would say if he knew that one of the play-actresses of whom he so heartily disapproved not only appeared on a stage but actually without a skirt.

Her expression must have shown what she was thinking, because Freddie said with a smile:

"You are not the only person who is shocked, Pandora; women often swoon in the audience when they see Madame Vestris and Kitty prancing about in their breeches."

"I expect I am old-fashioned," Pandora said.

She rose from the table and walked towards the door. As she reached it she said:

"Please ... will you tell ... Miss King about ... Norvin?"

She saw by his expression that it was not a task which he fancied, but he smiled at her and answered:

"I will, but it is an extraordinary thing that if there is any dirty work to do it is always I who have to do it!"

Pandora heard the other men chaffing him as she hurried upstairs.

She went to the Earl's room and beckoned Mrs. Meadowfield out into the corridor so that they could speak without having to lower their voices.

"The guests are all leaving as soon as everything is packed," she said.

"That's good news, Miss Pandora," Mrs. Meadowfield replied. "We don't want anyone disturbing His Lordship, do we?"

"No, of course not," Pandora agreed, "and I think, Mrs. Meadowfield, the snuff-boxes which have been neglected while you have been away need cleaning."

She did not need to say any more: she could see by the expression on Mrs. Meadowfield's face that she understood exactly what she meant.

As the Housekeeper hurried away down the passage, Pandora went into the Earl's bed-room.

He was lying as she had left him, but she thought his face was paler still than it had been before, and there was blood already beginning to seep through the clean linen with which the Doctor had bandaged his head.

She sat down beside the bed.

How could it be possible, she wondered, that in so short a time she could have lost her heart completely to a man who stood for everything that her uncle the Bishop of Lindchester thought of as wicked and evil?

She could understand what he had felt when his father had been allowed to die because there had been no help from any of the Charts.

She could also understand how bitterly her grandfather had hated anyone, whoever it might be, who would take the place of his beloved son George.

She tried to imagine what the Earl had done in London when he had inherited a huge fortune and because he hated the Charts had been determined to dissipate it.

She had only to think of Kitty still sleeping next door to know that he had turned instinctively to women who were denounced as outrageous and immoral, women, as her aunt had said, in whose company no decent man would be seen.

He had meant to behave indecently and he had succeeded, but now it was not Kitty King who had been instrumental in his being injured in a duel, but Pandora herself.

As if her thought of Kitty conjured up the actress, Pandora heard her speaking loudly and angrily outside in the passage. A moment later there was a loud knock on the door.

Hastily Pandora opened it, and found Kitty arguing with Freddie, who was obviously trying to prevent her from entering the Earl's bed-room.

"You are not going to keep him from me," she said furiously, and added as Pandora appeared: "Nor you either, you milk-faced, so-called cousin!"

Pandora shut the door behind her and stood against it.

Kitty was wearing only an elaborate lace-trimmed wrap over her nightgown and her face was not yet painted, powdered, or mascaraed.

Even so, with her red hair untidy and her lips their natural colour, she looked very attractive.

Her skin was blotchy from excessive drinking and there were dark lines under her eyes, but she was still exceptionally lovely and Pandora could understand why the Earl was infatuated with her.

Aloud she said calmly:

"You have been told that my cousin was injured in a duel? Sir Gilbert shot him in the head and the Doctor says he must have complete quiet."

"I don't believe you!" Kitty snarled. "It's a trick of yours to keep me away from him."

"You can see for yourself," Pandora answered. "But I beg of you, if you have any feelings at all for him, do not speak or make a noise."

She thought Kitty was going to say something rude, but as Pandora opened the door quickly and stepped inside the darkened room, Kitty followed her towards the great four-poster bed in which all the heads of the family had slept since the reign of Charles II.

It was so tall that the ostrich-feathers above the carved and gilded posts almost touched the painted ceiling.

Emblazoned on the velvet back was the colourful coat-of-arms of the family with its innumerable armorial bearings.

Kitty approached the bed and for once it seemed she was awed into silence. After staring at the Earl for a few seconds she turned and walked out of the room.

Freddie was waiting in the corridor.

"Is he going to die?" Kitty asked abruptly.

"We hope not."

"It looks to me as if he'll be ill for a long time."

"There is always that possibility," Freddie agreed.

"I suppose you'd better take me back to London."

"It would be wise," he said, "and, as I have already told you, there are rehearsals for you to think about."

Kitty was considering, then she made up her mind and looked at Pandora.

"All right," she said harshly, "you win! But I'm not leaving here without money. Only God knows how I'm going to manage until he's well again."

Pandora looked at Freddie in perplexity.

He raised his eye-brows in an expressive gesture which told her that she would not get rid of Kitty unless she gave her what she required.

"How ... how much do you ... want?" Pandora enquired.

"As much as I can get!" Kitty replied. "At least one hundred pounds."

"One hundred pounds?"

It seemed to her an immense sum of money and she thought wildly that it would be impossible, even if they were willing to do so, to provide so much.

Then she remembered that Michael Farrow, now that he was the agent, could draw on the Estate account.

She thought perhaps she should argue with Kitty and say that she was asking too much. Then she knew that Kitty would not lower her demand.

"I will see if that sum is available," she replied curtly. "In the meantime, will you ring for a maid to pack for you?"

"Very much the 'Lady of the Manor' at the moment, aren't you?" Kitty said with a sneer. "Well, make the most of it while he's too weak to say what he wants. He'll be back to me as soon as he can put a foot to the ground. Make no mistake about that!"

She walked into her bed-room as she spoke and slammed the door behind her.

"Can you manage to find one hundred pounds?" Freddie asked. "It seems a silly question in a place like this, but I know she will not budge without it."

"I will find it somehow," Pandora replied.

She went back into the Earl's bed-room and rang the bell.

It was answered by his valet, a man who looked to Pandora to be as sensible as the Doctor had said he was.

"Will you find Mr. Michael Farrow?" Pandora asked. "He may be in the Estate office. If not, send a groom to discover where he is. I have to speak to him immediately."

"Very good, Miss."

He looked towards the bed.

"His Lordship all right?"

"I think so. There is nothing more we can do for him until the Doctor comes back at noon."

"That's what I understood," the valet said. "Is there anything I can bring you, Miss?"

"Not for the moment, thank you."

He left, and Pandora walked back to her chair at the side of the bed.

Kitty's words were ringing in her ears and she was sure in her heart that the actress was right.

When he was well enough the Earl would either want to go to London or would bring Kitty back here.

'She is lovely,' Pandora thought with a little sigh, and except for when she was drunk she had a *joie de vivre* which would amuse and fascinate any man.

'How could I be like that?' she asked herself silently.

She remembered how little she knew about men and how ignorant she was of the amusements of London. She was certain that they were far more entertaining to someone like the Earl than anything Chart could offer.

It was an effort to tell herself that that was the truth, but she had to face it.

One day she had managed to interest him in the workings of the great Estate, but she had not forgotten the surprise in his voice when he asked her if she expected him to live permanently in the country.

How could she expect him to feel as she did about Chart? Or to enjoy riding and hunting as her father had?

She looked at the Earl lying unconscious beside her and she wanted to go down on her knees and ask him to give himself a real chance to understand and to love Chart.

Then she told herself that he would be lonely even with Chart, unless he had someone with whom to share it, and that someone, she was certain, would be Kitty or a woman like her.

She heard a soft knock on the door and the valet entered.

"Mr. Farrow is downstairs in the Morning-Room, Miss."

"Will you stay with His Lordship?" Pandora asked. "I will not be long."

"He'll be safe with me, Miss, however long you are."

"I am sure of that," Pandora answered.

She ran along the corridor and down the Great Staircase.

Michael Farrow, looking large, solid, and trustworthy, was standing by the fireplace.

"I'm sorry to hear what has happened, Miss Pandora. How is His Lordship?"

"Dr. Graham says he should be all right in a few days," Pandora answered, "but it is frightening to see him so quiet and still."

"I can understand that," Michael Farrow said sympathetically.

"I wanted to see you," Pandora told him, "for two reasons. One is that I need one hundred pounds immediately."

"Immediately?" Michael Farrow questioned, obviously surprised.

Then, as if he understood, he added quickly:

"I'll manage it somehow, but there'll be no time to go to the Bank in Lindchester."

"Then borrow it from anyone who will lend it to you," Pandora said, "and when you have it, hand it to Miss King."

"I'll do that, Miss Pandora."

"The other thing I was going to suggest," Pandora said, "is that your father, if he would, should go to London and close up Chart House."

Again she saw surprise in Michael Farrow's eyes, and she explained frankly:

"Things, as you know already, have a way of being stolen or of disappearing when they are not properly looked after. The Earl is ill, and anyway it is the end of the Season."

She drew in her breath as she went on:

"I am taking it upon myself to suggest that your father should pay off the servants who were not in the employ of my grandfather and also should check what is missing before they leave."

She did not say openly to Michael Farrow that she thought Kitty might in the Earl's absence help herself to anything valuable that took her fancy.

She was quite certain Kitty would have tried to take the snuff-boxes when she left Chart Hall.

Michael Farrow did not speak for a moment. Then he said:

"I wonder, Miss Pandora, if you'd think it a good idea if my father took Mr. Winslow with him to check the contents?"

"Mr. Winslow?" Pandora questioned.

Then she remembered that he had been the Headmaster of the big school in Lindchester until he had retired to the village, and her parents had found him to be a very intelligent man.

"He often tells my father how interested he is

in the history of Chart Hall and the family collection," Michael Farrow explained.

Pandora's eyes lit up.

Here, perhaps, was the Curator she had been hoping to find.

She gave her wholehearted approval to Michael Farrow's suggestion, and feeling that everything was being handled satisfactorily she went back to the Earl's bed-room.

Dr. Graham arrived at noon and found that there was no change in his patient.

Pandora was walking with him down the stairs when she saw that everybody was gathered in the hall ready for departure.

The Phaetons were waiting outside, while the luggage was being strapped onto the back of them.

The actresses looked as they had when they arrived, gaudily garbed in their taffeta capes and feather-bedecked bonnets.

They created a kaleidoscope of colour which seemed very alien to the dignity and good taste of the great Chart Hall.

Instinctively Pandora stopped when she saw who was waiting below, and she would not have proceeded had not the Doctor continued to walk down the stairs and she felt she must go with him.

"We are just waiting to say good-bye, Pandora," Freddie said, moving away from the chattering actresses, "but we heard that the Doctor was with you."

"He is just leaving," Pandora replied.

She introduced Dr. Graham and Freddie said:

"I hope His Lordship will soon be well. I am sure if you need a second opinion you will not hesitate to send for a London Physician."

"I have already thought of that," Dr. Graham replied, "and I intend to discuss it with Miss Stratton."

"Then I am sure my friend is in good hands," Freddie said.

The men came to say good-bye to Pandora and Caro did the same. Only Hettie and Kitty, who had been whispering together, looked at her with un-veiled enmity.

She knew that Kitty at any rate suspected her of having designs on the Earl.

"You can tell Norvin as soon as he can listen," Kitty said in a loud voice, "that I'll be expecting him and if he doesn't hurry up I'll not be waiting too long."

"That's not a very encouraging message to send to a sick man," Lottie protested.

Kitty tossed her head.

"Norvin knows he's not the only pebble on the beach."

"But most pebbles are not so generous," Hettie said in what was meant to be a low voice, but Pandora heard.

Again Kitty tossed her head, making the ostrich-feathers in her bonnet dance.

"I'm not playing 'Weeping Widow' for any man for long," she said, "and mind you get that into His Lordship's head!"

She added the last words furiously to Pandora.

Then, without waiting for an answer, she swept across the hall and climbed into a Phaeton which fortunately was large enough to hold three.

"We're going to race you!" Caro cried. "I bet you ten guineas that Richard and I reach Tyburn Hill before you do."

"Done!" Kitty screamed. "But make it ten guineas and a champagne supper."

"We'll win that!" Lottie said to Clive.

"Freddie's horses are better than mine," Clive replied.

"But there's three of them in the Phaeton and Kitty has more luggage than any of us."

"Well, we will have a damned good try," Clive said, "but do not count the guineas until they are in your hand."

"Come on and don't waste time!" Caro screamed.

Then they were all driving off, shouting and yelling at one another as they went.

As the last Phaeton crossed the bridge, Pandora gave a sigh of relief that came from the depths of her heart.

She thought that the Doctor would leave, but instead he walked towards the Morning-Room, saying:

"I want a word with you, Pandora."

She followed him into the room in which she had first met the Earl, and she felt for a moment that she could still see him lying back in her grandfather's chair, his leg over the arm of it.

How could she have guessed, how could she have known, that she would fall in love with him?

"Now, Pandora," Dr. Graham said, "I think you had better tell me what you intend to do."

His question came as a surprise.

"I want to stay . . . here and . . . nurse my cousin," Pandora answered.

"Alone, with no chaperon?"

"You can hardly look on the women who have just left as chaperons," Pandora replied.

"I am wondering what your mother would say about your being in this house at all."

"There was nothing else I could do," Pandora said in a low voice. "Uncle Augustus intended to . . . marry me off to his Chaplain."

"To Prosper Witheridge?" the Doctor asked.

"You have met him?"

"Once or twice at meetings in Lindchester."

"Then you know what he is like," Pandora said. "He is horrible and I hate him. How could I contemplate marrying such a man?"

"So you asked your cousin to save you from such an alliance!"

"I knew that if I stayed here, Prosper Witheridge would be so shocked he would not offer for me, and that is exactly what has happened."

"Well, desperate ills sometimes need desperate remedies," Dr. Graham remarked. "But what does the Bishop say about all this?"

"Uncle Augustus does not return from London until today," Pandora said in a low voice.

The Doctor did not speak and after a moment she went on:

"I expect he will see me and tell me I am to return. If he does, would you ... would you tell him that I am ... needed here?"

The Doctor moved restlessly.

"Quite frankly, I do not know the answer to that question, Pandora," he said. "I am well aware of the way in which His Lordship is regarded in Lindchester and of course in the village of Chart."

"Things will be better now."

Dr. Graham smiled.

"I have heard how you persuaded him to sack that ghastly man Anstey and reinstate Farrow. When I was told what had happened and also how you took him to call on the farmers, I felt it was just the sort of thing your mother would have done."

"I am sure she was ... helping me to do what was ... right," Pandora said simply.

"And do you really think your mother would wish you to stay here?"

Pandora made a little gesture and asked:

"What is the alternative? To go back to Lindchester? Even if Mr. Witheridge will no longer want me to be his wife, my aunt will make my life a misery that I cannot describe."

There were tears in her eyes as she added:

"Oh, Dr. Graham, I have been so unhappy there, and not only through losing Mama and Papa. That was bad enough, but to live with hatred, incessant fault-finding, and knowing that everything I do is wrong, is a purgatory far worse than anything Prosper Witheridge could devise."

She spoke with a passionate intensity which moved the Doctor.

He put his arm round her shoulders and said:

"I have been fond of you, Pandora, ever since you were a little girl. I was intensely proud to count your father and mother as my friends. Whatever happens, you can always rely on me to do what I can for you."

"Do you mean that?" Pandora asked. "It is so kind that I do not know how to thank you."

"It is, however, difficult to know what I can do," the Doctor said gravely, "but I will think of something."

"I cannot go back to the Palace . . . I cannot!" Pandora said.

"I will wait and see what your uncle has to say about it," the Doctor said. "But surely there are other relations who would look after you?"

"If there are, they have certainly ignored me since Mama and Papa died," Pandora replied.

She sighed and added:

"If only I could get some work of some sort, perhaps nursing an old lady, or looking after small children."

"That is more or less the sort of thing I had in mind," the Doctor replied.

He gave her an affectionate hug, then he said:

"I have half a dozen patients waiting to see me, and it is doubtful if I shall get any luncheon, but I will come back at about five o'clock."

"Perhaps Norvin will be better by then," Pandora said optimistically. "And thank you, Dr. Graham, for all your kindness. I knew you would understand."

"More than anyone else will," the Doctor said ruefully. "But even the most assiduous muck-raker must agree that a man who is unconscious can hardly constitute a danger to a young girl."

"I am in no danger from Cousin Norvin."

She wanted to add: "Unfortunately!" but instead she walked to the front door with the Doctor and said good-bye.

When he had driven away she ran upstairs feeling suddenly joyful and excited because there were no more enemies in the house with whom to contend. For a few hours at any rate she had the Earl to herself.

She sat in the darkened room all the afternoon and because she was tired she fell asleep for a little while.

She awoke with a feeling of guilt because she

thought she had not kept watch over her patient as adequately as she should have done.

She looked at the clock and calculated that about this time her uncle and aunt should be arriving back from London.

She could imagine their being greeted by Prosper Witheridge and she knew that he would in his own way be delighted that he had her misdeeds to relate to them.

She was quite certain that he would never forgive her for saying that she hated him and had no wish to marry him.

He would take his revenge by exaggerating everything that had happened at Chart Hall, and she was certain that his description of the actresses would lose nothing in the telling.

"It will take uncle Augustus at least an hour to listen to all that," Pandora said to herself. "Then he will doubtless want to change and have something to eat and drink, so it is unlikely he will be here before half past six, or perhaps seven o'clock."

She looked at the silent Earl and said:

"I need you! I need you to fight for me and protect me."

As she spoke she admitted that she had always hoped at the back of her mind that when the time came he would defy her uncle as he had defied Prosper Witheridge.

Then she knew almost despairingly that the situation was very different.

He uncle was her Guardian. Whatever the Earl might say, the Bishop had a greater right to decide her life than did a distant cousin.

"I am a Chart," Pandora said aloud. "The Strattons are so very different from anything I feel or am. Papa himself found them bores and avoided his relatives whenever he could. Why then should I be forced to obey them?"

As if the idea was so agitating, she rose from the big arm-chair in which she had slept and walked across the room to one of the three windows.

The curtains were drawn and she slipped behind them so that she could look out through the window.

The gardens were bathed in sunshine glinting golden on the lake and making the colours of the flowers seem almost dazzling.

"I belong here!" Pandora said aloud. "This is where my roots are."

It suddenly struck her that she would rather die than return to Lindchester. If she drowned herself in the lake or threw herself off the roof, then she would remain at Chart however much anyone tried to take her from it.

Then she knew she had no wish to die. She wanted to live, she wanted to live for the Earl, even if he never cared for her except in the casual manner he had shown so far.

He had teased her, argued with her, defied her, and yet every moment, every second, she had been with him had been an inexpressible delight.

'Perhaps if I offered to work in the still-room or in the gardens he would let me stay,' she thought. 'He need never see me unless he wished to do so, but I would be here and it would be wonderful to be near him.'

She went back into the room and now as she moved towards the bed, adjusting her eyes from the sunshine to the dimness, she had the idea that perhaps she could communicate her longing and love to his subconscious mind.

She reached the bed and knelt down beside him.

"I love you! And I want you to love Chart. I ask nothing for myself except that I may stay here, where I belong, because I know that one day Chart will give you happiness if only you will let it."

She spoke with such intensity that tears came into her eyes.

But the Earl did not move and she thought in desperation that he could not hear her and time was ticking on so that soon her uncle would come and take her away.

She knew that if he insisted on her returning

with him there was really nothing she could do but obey, for it was very doubtful that he would listen to Dr. Graham, whom he would despise as an unimportant country Doctor.

'Once I am back at the Palace, Norvin will forget about me,' she thought, 'and when he returns to London there will be Kitty waiting for him.'

She felt as if she stuck a dagger into her heart and twisted it.

There was no use pretending, she thought. Kitty would be waiting, and however drunk and vulgar she might appear, she would still amuse him, still be the type of woman whom the Earl, Freddie, Richard, and Clive all preferred.

Pandora rose from her knees and as she did so the door opened and Mrs. Meadowfield returned.

"I've had a nice rest, Miss Pandora," she said in a whisper. "Now you go out in the garden and get some fresh air. It's not right for you to be cooped up in here when it's such a lovely day. Burrows has laid tea for you in the Salon, so have a cup first. It'll do you good."

Pandora felt touched that the servants were thinking of her.

But, it made her remember with a shudder that her aunt with her fault-finding and her punishments of making her repeat everything two or three times would be getting ready for her return to the Palace.

The tea-table was laid, in all its glittering glory, by the window, and the sunshine came pouring in over the terrace as Pandora drank the fragrant China tea which her mother had preferred to any other.

She ate one of the sandwiches; then, finding them delicious and cut almost paper-thin, she took two more from the plate and walked through the French-window into the garden.

She remembered how she had done the same thing last night, an action which had resulted in Sir Gilbert challenging the Earl to the duel from which he was now suffering.

'So much has happened since I came here,' Pandora thought with a sigh.

She walked across the velvet-like lawns and into the rose-garden. The sun-dial was very ancient and she leant against it, wondering how many Charts had done so before her.

"Perhaps they were as frightened and apprehensive over their future as I am," Pandora told herself, "but whatever happened, it did not really matter because when they died, Chart went on living."

She tried to convince herself that it would not matter what happened to her. But she knew that she longed to live, to experience all the emotions that were possible for a human being, and most of all love.

It was impossible for her thoughts not to keep returning to the Earl.

She kept remembering the sensations she had felt when he held her in his arms on the horse and she had been so close against him that she could feel his heart beating.

Could anything seem more reprehensible to her uncle and aunt than that she should be abducted when she was wearing nothing but a thin dressing-gown over her nightgown?

They would be appalled that she had been so close to the Earl that she had been able to hide her face against his shoulder.

But there had been nothing wrong about it, Pandora thought to herself. It had been right and somehow good at that moment. Good as Prosper Witheridge might be, he would never understand, nor would Aunt Sophie nor Uncle Augustus.

The Earl had been like a Knight saving her from destruction. Yet, those who abused him were so convinced that everything he did was evil that they could never imagine him doing anything good.

She thought now of how he had come to her bed-room to save her from Sir Gilbert.

It was the first time she had considered that the world would think it very reprehensible that he, the wicked Earl, had come into her room and she had not screamed for him to leave it.

"I did not think of him as a man ... then," she told herself.

But now he was a man with every breath he drew—a man she loved.

'Everything is really in the mind,' Pandora reasoned in her mind, touching the sun-dial with her fingers.

Some words of Milton came to her and she felt that she longed to say them to the Earl:

The mind is its own place, and in itself
Can make a Heav'n of Hell, a Hell of Heav'n.

"It is the mind that counts," Pandora said aloud, "and not always one's actions."

Only the Earl would understand her reasoning, and she longed to tell him what she had thought out for herself:

"'A Heav'n of Hell, a Hell of Heav'n.' That is what I want him to find at Chart ... a Heaven where he had previously thought it Hell, in his hatred of everything for which it stands."

She clasped her hands together and whispered:

"I will make him understand ... I will make him realise how he can ... change the past into a new ... future."

Because she felt she could not wait to see him again, Pandora ran back to the house.

Then as she walked from the Salon into the hall, preparatory to going upstairs, she came to a standstill and felt as if she had turned to stone.

The front door was open and outside she could see a carriage she recognised.

She had been expecting her uncle, but now that he was here she was desperately afraid.

She felt like a child who had been caught out in doing something incredibly naughty and knew there was no escape from the punishment it entailed.

Feeling that she must have gone very pale, her fingers were cold; Pandora waited.

Then, to her astonishment, instead of seeing her uncle's tall, gaunt figure coming up the steps, Burrows, who had gone to the door of the carriage, returned alone, holding something in his hand.

He took a silver salver from where it was standing on a side-table and came towards Pandora.

"A note for you, Miss."

For a moment it was difficult for Pandora to move, then with an effort she took the note from the salver and went back into the Salon.

It was such a relief not to see her uncle, to know that he had not come in person as she had expected, that it was hard to think of anything else.

She could only stare at what she held in her hand, recognising the strong, upright writing in which he had inscribed her name, and thinking at the eleventh hour she had escaped being decapitated.

She opened the envelope.

The writing danced in front of her eyes, then she forced herself to read what was written there.

My Dear Niece:

Your Aunt and I have returned from London to learn from Mr. Prosper Witheridge of your outrageous and unforgiveable behaviour as soon as our backs were turned.

I cannot credit that any decently brought up girl should act in such an unconventional and deceitful manner which could only bring deserved retribution in its train.

Your Aunt and I have discussed your behaviour, which has given us deep distress, and we have decided regretfully that in the circumstances we cannot invite you to return here to us at the Palace.

My Chaplain informs me that your behaviour is already being talked about in

Lindchester, and to condone such behaviour would involve me personally and certainly your Aunt in a situation I can only describe as extremely unpleasant.

I can therefore only hope that your Chart relations are prepared to offer you a home and see to your welfare, as we have attempted to do.

It is with a feeling both of distress and of personal failure that I leave you to your conscience and to the mercy of God.

Pandora read the letter wide-eyed. Then, as if she could hardly believe the information she had received, she read it again.

She was free! Her uncle had relinquished his hold over her and abandoned her to her fate!

It was what she had wanted, and yet somehow she felt a little frightened now that it had actually happened.

Now she was alone, completely alone, in a manner in which she had never before been alone in the whole of her life.

Then she saw that there was something else included in the letter. It was a piece of paper and when she opened it she saw that it was a cheque.

She stared in surprise until she realised that it was made out for forty-two pounds and must be exactly what was left of her father and mother's money.

She realised that the Bishop had deducted all expenses for the funeral and she was sure a certain sum for her keep since she had been at the Palace.

But at least she was not entirely penniless.

Holding the letter and cheque in her hand, she left the Salon and walked slowly up the stairs.

Mrs. Meadowfield was ready to leave the Earl as soon as Pandora appeared.

She came out into the passage to say:

"I thought you'd like to know, Miss, that the ladies who were staying here asked the maids to include all sorts of things in their luggage which was not theirs."

"I rather expected that, Mrs. Meadowfield," Pandora said gravely.

"Like magpies, they were," Mrs. Meadowfield said scathingly. "Cushion-covers, lace face-towels, and ornaments off the dressing-tables what have been here for years—all would have been removed if they'd had their way."

She paused before going on indignantly:

"And that Miss King had even secreted in her hand-bag three of the miniatures from the Countess's room."

"She was not allowed to take them, Mrs. Meadowfield?" Pandora asked in alarm.

"No, Miss. Fortunately, she left her hand-bag behind when she went to another lady's room, and I've put them back on the wall where they belong."

"Oh, thank you, thank you," Pandora said. "I knew you would understand when I mentioned the snuff-boxes."

"Miss King asked me where they were," Mrs. Meadowfield said, "and I told her they had all gone to be repaired. There was nothing she could do about them then."

"No, indeed," Pandora agreed.

However much the Earl might think it was interfering, she was glad that she had saved the treasures of Chart Hall.

She was also certain that Mr. Farrow, once he reached London, would prevent anything from being stolen from Chart House.

"Those women are as unscrupulous and dishonest as Dalton and Mr. Anstey!" she told herself as she went to the Earl's bed-room.

She wished that she could tell him what had happened, but she knew it would be wiser if she said nothing.

He might resent her interference, and if it suited him he would be quite prepared to say that he wished to give Kitty and the other women anything they wanted to have.

She could still hear him saying that he would leave nothing but the bare walls for his successors.

It struck her that if he was so ready to dispose of the contents of Chart Hall, he would be even more ready to dispose of her.

For a moment she had thought his hatred of the family had evaporated because of what she had told him about her mother's desire to help. Yet, she could be sure of nothing—least of all what he felt about her.

Once again she went to kneel at his side.

Because he was so still and silent she had a sudden, terrifying fear that he might have died without her being aware of it.

Frightened, she put out her hand and slipped it through his nightshirt to feel his heart.

It was beating; then, as she felt it throb against the palm of her hand, she felt a thrill run through her which was even more intense than it had been before.

"I love you . . . and I . . . belong to you!" she said beneath her breath.

"I belong to you whether you wish it or not . . . and I shall never love . . . anyone else! Because you are you . . . you fill my . . . whole life, now and forever. . . ."

It was almost in the nature of a vow, and as her words died away in the silence of the bed-room Pandora knew they were true.

She had laid herself completely and absolutely at his feet and nothing he could say or do could ever alter that.

Chapter Seven

"Thank you, Farrow, I will see you tomorrow," the Earl said. "I hope to be up by then."

"I hope so too, M'Lord," Michael Farrow replied.

He picked up from the bed the papers they had been discussing, bowed, and left.

As soon as the door closed behind him the Earl looked into the far corner of the room and clicked his fingers.

Instantly something small, swift, and agile jumped onto the bed to lie beside him, licking his hand and ingratiating herself with every movement of her body.

The Earl fondled the soft ears of the spaniel.

"I suppose you know you are going to get into a lot of trouble for being on the satin cover."

His voice only seemed to excite the dog further and she licked the Earl's hand in a fervour of admiration.

It was the first thing the Earl had known on coming back to consciousness from what he learnt afterwards was three days of delirium.

Hazily he had wondered who could be kissing his hand; then, looking down, he saw the brown eyes of a small black and white spaniel.

"Her name is Juno," a quiet voice said, and he saw Pandora rise from where she had been sitting by the window.

"Who said I wanted a dog?" the Earl enquired

drowsily, but as he asked the question he knew the answer.

It was another chain to link him to Chart.

Pandora did not reply. She stood looking down at him and he thought she had the same expression in her eyes as Juno did.

She had in fact called on every Keeper on the Estate before she found a dog which she thought would suit the Earl.

She had known from the moment she took Juno into the sick-room that her choice had been a wise one.

The bitch seemed to understand exactly what was expected of her. She settled herself down beside the bed as if she knew she was waiting for her master to awaken.

Almost despite himself the Earl in the last few days had found it impossible to resist her blandishments, and despite all Pandora's admonishings Juno would jump onto the bed when there was no-one else in the room.

Now, with a hearing that was more acute than the Earl's, she slipped back onto the floor and into the corner from where she had come a second before the door opened.

Pandora came in, carrying in her hands a tall vase of Madonna lilies.

"I was waiting for Michael Farrow to go," she said, "to bring you these. They are so lovely and smell divine."

"And are therefore most inappropriate for a sinner like myself," the Earl said mockingly. "You should keep them in your own room, Pandora. I have always been told they are the emblem of saintliness."

Ever since he had been well enough to do so he had teased her, and they duelled with words as they had before.

As Pandora set the lilies down on one of the inlaid chest of drawers he went on:

"Farrow has been telling me how busy you have been since I was laid up."

Pandora stiffened a little nervously.

She had not told him anything she had done after the duel, reasoning to herself that it was because she did not wish him to be troubled.

But if she was honest she knew that it was because she was afraid he would think she was interfering.

"You sent old Farrow to close the London house," the Earl said, and she thought his voice was accusing.

"It was the ... end of the Season," Pandora answered in a low voice, "and I thought it was ... unnecessary for you to employ so ... many servants when you were ... unlikely to go there until it is ... cooler."

"The Theatres are still open in London."

The Earl spoke the words deliberately and watched Pandora's face.

He saw the colour rise in her cheeks, but she turned away so that all he could see was the back of her head as she walked towards the window.

"It will be quite ... easy to ... reopen the house."

"You arranged for someone called Winslow to make an inventory, so Farrow tells me. He has marked in items that are missing. I expect you would like to see it."

"It ... it is not my ... business," Pandora replied.

"No?" the Earl questioned. "I thought you would be concerned."

She did not speak, and after a moment he went on:

"Farrow was also telling me how difficult it was to find the money which Kitty required before she left. He even had to borrow ten pounds of it from the Vicar."

He laughed as he added:

"That was certainly a case of the Church providing the damned with more than a drop of water."

Pandora turned round.

"Please, do not ... talk like ... that," she pleaded.

"You may have ... thought it wrong of me ... but otherwise she would ... have refused to go, and it was ... essential that you should not be ... disturbed."

"And as you so rightly thought, she was a disturbing influence."

Again the Earl's voice was mocking.

"I am ... sorry if anything I did was ... wrong," Pandora murmured. "I knew I should not intrude ... but in the ... circumstances I thought I was ... doing what was ... best."

"From your point of view—or mine?" the Earl enquired.

"From yours, of course," Pandora answered. "It had nothing to do with me."

"Chart had nothing to do with you?" the Earl queried. "Now really, Saint Pandora, what you are saying comes perilously near to being a lie."

Pandora clasped her hands together.

"I love Chart ... you know I ... love it!" she said. "But it is yours, your house ... your Estate ... your Kingdom!"

The Earl smiled.

"My Milton is coming back to me. What you are saying is: I am 'as he who seeking asses, found a kingdom.' "

"Have you found it?" Pandora enquired.

She spoke with an intensity that surprised herself. Then she knew it was the question she had been longing to ask him ever since he had been well enough to take an interest in what was happening round him, to see Farrow, and to give orders.

The Earl held out his hand.

"Come here, Pandora," he said. "I want to talk to you."

Almost as if she was reluctant and nervous, she moved very slowly a few steps towards him before she said:

"If you are ... well enough, I want to ... talk to you."

"I am well enough," the Earl said positively, "so

why not now? And as we both have something to say
to each other, I must play the gentleman and concede
to a lady the right to go first."

Pandora sat down in the chair that was placed
near the bed for anyone who wished to talk to the
Earl.

She did not look at him but sat staring at her
linked fingers as if she had never seen them before.

The Earl's eyes were on her face and after a few
seconds had passed he said:

"I am waiting, and of course I am extremely
curious to hear what you have to say to me."

"You may ... perhaps have ... wondered," Pandora said in a hesitating little voice, "why ... Uncle
Augustus has permitted me to ... stay here after he
returned from London."

"It had crossed my mind," the Earl replied. "But,
as you were nursing me so efficiently, I presumed he
thought that prostrate and unconscious I hardly con-
stituted a danger to your youth and innocence."

"Uncle Augustus did not ... come to see me ...
himself," Pandora went on. "I expected him to do so
... but instead he ... wrote me a ... letter."

The Earl did not speak and after a moment
she said:

"He told me that I had ... caused so much ...
scandal in Lindchester by ... coming here that he
and my aunt could no longer ... offer me a home with
... them."

The Earl raised his eye-brows. Then he said:

"It is an action you might have anticipated—in
fact you did anticipate it when you came here to
escape the advances of the fire-breathing Chaplain."

His lips twisted in a faint smile as he added:

"What were the words you told me which made
you think of such a solution to your problem? Something about my never entertaining anything but doxies and play-actresses with whom no decent man
would associate."

Pandora made a little sound but she did not inter-
rupt as the Earl continued:

"You chose to make your descent into Hell. You can hardly blame the pontifical Bishop if he feels you have become slightly besmirched in the process."

"I am not . . . complaining," Pandora replied, "but I have to make some . . . plans for the . . . future. That is why I wanted to . . . ask you . . . something."

"What is that?" the Earl enquired.

"I thought . . . perhaps if you would . . . allow me I . . . could stay . . . here."

She glanced at him for a moment, then went on quickly:

"Not as a guest, not as an encumbrance in any way. You need never see me, but I could work in the still-room or help Mrs. Meadowfield by mending the linen. There are dozens of things I could do . . . and you would not even . . . know I was . . . here."

"And you think that would make you happy?" the Earl asked.

"To be at Chart Hall would be like being in Heaven!" Pandora answered, and her face lit up. "I promise on my honour I would not do anything that you would find irritating or obtrusive . . . but I would be here . . . and sometimes I could see—"

She stopped suddenly.

She had been so carried away by what she was saying that she had forgotten that if she finished her sentence it would be very revealing.

She might have guessed, however, that such an observation would not escape the Earl.

"You would see . . . ?" he questioned. "What or whom?"

Pandora hesitated.

"The . . . people in the . . . village, of . . . whom I am very . . . fond."

"Of course," the Earl agreed. "And you do not think you would find it encumbent upon you to remonstrate with me if I brought my dissolute friends down from London, smashing, stealing, or disposing of things that you would consider to be sacred because they have been in the family for so many years?"

"I should mind . . . of course I should mind," Pandora replied honestly, "but you would not be . . . aware of my . . . feelings."

"Just because you did not express them?" the Earl queried. "You do not think I would feel your condemnation vibrating through the Castle, standing behind me like the voice of my conscience, dragging me out of the depths of my depravity?"

"I would try not to . . . make you . . . feel like . . . that."

"Supposing I tell you that however much you tried, I should be aware of your thoughts, your feelings, and your unhappiness."

"What you are . . . really saying," Pandora said in a very low voice, "is that you do not . . . want me . . . here."

"I have not said that."

"It is . . . what you . . . mean," she insisted, "and I . . . understand."

She gave a little sigh and he saw that her fingers were trembling, but her voice had a note of bravery in it as she went on:

"Dr. Graham said he would try to find me . . . employment of . . . some sort, but perhaps it would be . . . best if I went . . . away from Chart altogether."

"Surely that would be very selfish."

"Selfish?"

"Who is going to teach me the history of the family if you are not here? Who is going to remind me how the last Earl, the Earl before him, and the Earl before that, behaved?"

"I . . . I do not . . . understand what you are . . . saying," Pandora replied. "You do not . . . want me here . . . and yet you say . . ."

"I have not said I do not want you," the Earl answered. "I merely said that however skilfully you hide yourself, if you are in the Castle I should feel your presence."

Pandora made a helpless little gesture with her hands, and her eyes looked at his piteously.

"Then . . . tell me what I am . . . to do."

He looked at her and it was impossible for either of them to look away.

Then, after a long moment when it seemed to Pandora that there was just the expression in the Earl's eyes and nothing else in the whole world, she said again in a whisper that was almost beneath her breath:

"I do not ... understand."

The Earl put out his hand again and now almost as if she was mesmerised into obeying him she put her hand into his.

He pulled her firmly towards him and she was not quite certain how it happened, but she was now sitting on the side of the bed, facing him, so close that his face was only a little way from hers.

"What I am trying to say, Pandora," the Earl said quietly, "is that if I am to stay at Chart, which is what you have been insisting I must do, then you must stay here with me."

He saw a sudden expression of hope in her eyes and he went on:

"Not in the still-room, not hidden away in some obscure part of the house, but with me."

He felt the sudden movement of Pandora's fingers as they fluttered in his, and now she was holding on to him, afraid that what she had heard was untrue or else she had misunderstood his meaning.

"If we are to live here together," the Earl went on, "it will certainly give Lindchester too much to talk about, unless you make an effort to bring an air of respectability to Chart Hall."

Pandora's eyes were still held by his.

"H-how ... could I ... do that?"

The words were hardly audible, but he heard them.

"Do I have to spell it out?" he questioned. "But of course! Every woman is entitled to the full drama of a proposal of marriage."

He saw the startled, astonished expression on Pandora's face and said very softly:

"Will you marry me, my lovely one? It will be

an ill-assorted union of the Saint and the Sinner, but perhaps we can compromise halfway between the two."

He spoke as if he forced himself to be light and mocking, but there was an expression in his eyes that made Pandora draw in her breath.

"D-do you mean ... do you really mean ... ?" she began.

Then the Earl's arms were round her as he pulled her roughly against him.

"I mean this," he said, and his lips came down on hers.

For a moment Pandora could hardly realise, hardly believe, that it was happening.

Then she knew that this was everything she wanted, everything she had longed and prayed for and thought was completely impossible and beyond her reach.

Her lips were very soft, young, and innocent, and the Earl instinctively checked his desire and kissed her gently until he felt her respond and her body quiver against his.

To Pandora the wonder of his lips evoked a thousand times more vividly and intensely the sensation she had experienced when she had felt his heart beating against the palm of her hand.

As he held her closer still, she knew that his lips gave her all the beauty of Chart, all her love of the great house and the things she had revered and treasured because she was a part of them.

Her whole body responded to his and she felt herself throbbing with the wonder and perfection of it.

Finally when the Earl raised his head to look down into her face she could only feel as if he lifted her up into the sky and it was impossible to come back to earth.

"I ... love ... you!" she whispered, and knew they were the words she had spoken a thousand times, but never had she thought she would be able to say them to him.

"What have you done to me, my darling?" the Earl asked, and his voice was very deep and moved. "I suppose I might have known this would happen when you first came into the Morning-Room looking so frightened and so incredibly lovely in your little Puritan dress."

"Do you ... really love ... me?" Pandora asked.

"I tried to hate you because you are a Chart, because you are one of my cursed relations," the Earl said. "I wanted you to be shocked and outraged by my friends and their behaviour. Instead, I have been unable to see anything but your face and your eyes. They have haunted me and captivated me as I am convinced they will do for the rest of my life."

"It is not true ... it cannot be true that you ... really want me," Pandora murmured.

Now, because it was all so overwhelming, the tears ran down her cheeks.

The Earl kissed them away. Then he was kissing her lips again, kissing her demandingly, passionately, as if he wanted to possess every particle of her and make it his own.

"I love you!" he said. "I love you so overwhelmingly that I, like you, cannot believe it is true that this is really happening. But it is, my precious, and I suppose you are going to say it is all due to some spell the Hall has cast upon us."

"Perhaps it is the house ... perhaps the people who have lived in it ... and perhaps it is just ... ourselves," Pandora answered, "but when I fell in ... love with you, I never ... thought that ... you would ... love me."

"And now you know that I do?" the Earl asked.

She hid her face against him because she felt it was impossible to answer him, impossible to explain the wild thrills that were running through her or that her heart was singing with some angelic chorus high above the earth.

The Earl kissed her hair.

"You smelt of violets when I carried you back on my horse after those swines had abducted you," he said, "and I knew then that that was the fragrance I wanted in my home and which was already in my heart."

"Oh, Norvin!" Pandora whispered, thinking of the strong perfume which Kitty and all the other actresses had used.

As if he sensed what she was thinking, as he always did, he said:

"Forget them. They served their purpose in bringing us together. Fate moves in mysterious ways!"

"If that is true," Pandora said, "I shall always be grateful, deeply ... deeply grateful, that they brought me ... here to you, but ... Norvin ... ?"

It was a question, and after a moment he asked: "What is it?"

"They are so ... pretty ... amusing, and entertaining ... and I am ... afraid that you will find me ... dull."

She did not look at him as she spoke, and the Earl smiled over her head as if he looked back into the past and realised it was a closed chapter.

Aloud he said:

"You may not have the footlights to glamourise you, my lovely one; you may not wear breeches and drink champagne until the early hours of the morning; but I have a feeling that the drama and romance of Chart will prove more entertaining than *The Beggar's Opera* or any other play."

His arms tightened as he added:

"I promise you no Leading Lady could be lovelier or more alluring than you."

She looked up at him with a smile of radiant happiness, then his lips were once more on hers.

He kissed her demandingly and insistently until she felt a flame within her respond to the fire in his eyes and the frantic beating of his heart that she could feel against her breasts.

Then with an effort she pushed him away from her and rose from the bed.

"You are ... supposed to be ... an invalid," she

said, her voice unsteady and breathless. "You must
. . . not exert yourself or get over-excited."

"I am over-excited!" he answered.

"Do . . . I . . . excite . . . you?"

"To the point of madness. I want to pull you into
bed with me and show you how much I love you."

He spoke passionately and saw the colour flare
into Pandora's cheeks. He laughed softly.

"My sweet darling, my precious, innocent little
Saint, I must not shock you!"

He would have pulled her back into his arms
but she avoided him and stood just out of reach, looking at him with her heart in her eyes.

He knew, as he saw her flushed cheeks, her lips
soft from his kisses, and her fair hair a little tumbled,
that he had never imagined a woman could look
more lovely or more enticing.

He held out both his arms to her.

"Come here! I want you!"

"You must be . . . sensible, and take . . . care of
yourself," Pandora replied.

Then as she was propelled towards him despite
herself, she moved forward not into his arms but onto
her knees beside him.

"Is it . . . true . . . is it really . . . true that you . . .
want me for your wife? It is what I have . . . longed
for, what Mama would have wished, that I should be
here in her home! But it is all too . . . wonderful for
me not to think it is a dream and I shall wake up."

"It is true, my sweet," the Earl answered, "but
you will have to help me. I have made a mess of
everything up-to-date—I am well aware of that—so I
need you! God knows I need you!"

Pandora leant her cheek against his hand as it
covered hers, and he went on:

"I suppose those are the same words that a man
says to a woman when he wants her body and her
love, but I want much more from you."

Pandora raised her face to look up at him.

Her eyes were full of sunshine.

"I have lived with hate for so long," the Earl continued, "that it is ingrained deep within me. It has coloured everything I have done, said, and thought."

He paused before he went on, his voice suddenly harsh:

"When I call myself a sinner I do not exaggerate, Pandora. I have done things of which I am ashamed. Things which I hope you will never know about, but nevertheless I cannot undo them, nor, I suppose, ever erase them completely from my conscience or what you would call my soul."

"You are ... forgiven," Pandora said softly.

"You are thinking of the joy in Heaven over a sinner that repenteth," the Earl said with a faint smile. "But I am not worrying about Heaven, Pandora, I am worrying about you."

His fingers tightened on hers as he said:

"You are so perfect, so good, and so pure that I am afraid."

"Of what?"

"That sooner or later you will turn away from me in disgust, that you will leave me because however much I try—'long is the way and hard, that out of hell leads up to light.'"

His voice died away on the quotation and she felt that he waited to hear her reply almost as if it were the voice of judgement and there was no escape from it.

Pandora rose from her knees to sit once more on the side of the bed and put her arms round him.

"You have forgotten ... something," she whispered.

"What have I forgotten?"

"That we have the only thing that matters ... the only thing that ... sweeps away darkness ... wickedness, and even the ... retribution of the past."

The Earl pulled her a little closer to him.

"Will our love really do that?"

"Do you doubt it?" Pandora asked. "Real love

... true love, has illuminated and sanctified those who have found it since the beginning of time."

"And that is the love we have for each other?" the Earl questioned.

"It is the way I love you," Pandora answered. "To me you have always been everything that is kind and good. I am not concerned with what happened before we met. The only thing I can think about is that we can be ... together in the ... future."

The Earl held her so closely that she could hardly breathe.

"We will be together," he said, "and, my perfect darling, I know that your love will give me not what I deserve but what I want."

"And will it be ... enough?"

"Could I want anything but you—and of course, a future Earl for Chart?" the Earl replied.

Because it was what she wanted to hear more than anything else, she lifted her face to his and kissed him.

In an instant the fire was there, holding her captive, and the Earl kissed her until the room swam dizzily round her with the wonder of it.

"I love ... you! Oh, Norvin ... how much I ... love you!" Pandora whispered brokenly. "But you ... must rest. ..."

Then, as if with a superhuman effort, she moved again from the security and safety of his arms to say accusingly:

"Look at Juno! I have told her she is not to come on the bed. Mrs. Meadowfield will be furious!"

The Earl laughed and looked down at the spaniel, which, jealous of not having the Earl's attention, was snuggling against him.

"What you are really worrying about," he said, his eyes twinkling, "is that Juno is spoiling the cover which was embroidered in the year-dot by some Chart who had nothing better to do."

"In 1706 to be exact!" Pandora replied. "This

cover was made by the wife of the second Earl when he was away at the wars with Marlborough."

She spoke automatically, then suddenly both she and the Earl were laughing.

"I realise that even when I am making love to you," he exclaimed, "you will still behave like a cross between a history- and a guide-book!"

She looked at him a little irresolutely, as if she was not certain whether he was merely amused or slightly annoyed. Then he took her hand in his and kissed it.

"I am a very willing pupil, my 'divinely fair' darling," he smiled, "as long as you will let me teach you one thing which is even more important than the history of all those virtuous and respectable Charts."

"What is . . . that?" Pandora asked.

"I will teach you to love me," he replied, "for however knowledgeable you are about some things, my adorable little Saint, I think on that subject I shall be the teacher and you the pupil."

"A very . . . willing and a very . . . humble pupil," Pandora whispered.

Then because she could not help herself she let him draw her into his arms again, and he was kissing her wildly, passionately, demandingly.

Outside, the sunshine turned the lake to gold and glittered on the windows of the great house which had throughout the centuries protected, inspired, and uplifted those who lived in it.

ABOUT THE AUTHOR

BARBARA CARTLAND, the world's most famous romantic novelist, who is also an historian, playwright, lecturer,
political speaker and television personality, has now written over 200 books. She has also had many historical
works published and has written four autobiographies as
well as the biographies of her mother and that of her
brother Ronald Cartland, who was the first Member of
Parliament to be killed in the last war. This book has a
preface by Sir Winston Churchill. Barbara Cartland has
sold 80 million books over the world, more than half of
these in the U.S.A. She broke the world record in 1975 by
writing twenty books, and her own record in 1976 with
twenty-one. In private life, Barbara Cartland, who is a
Dame of the Order of St. John of Jerusalem, has fought
for better conditions and salaries for Midwives and Nurses.
As President of the Royal College of Midwives (Hert-
fordshire Branch), she has been invested with the first
Badge of Office ever given in Great Britain, which was
subscribed to by the Midwives themselves. She has also
championed the cause for old people and founded the first
Romany Gypsy Camp in the world. Barbara Cartland is
deeply interested in Vitamin Therapy and is President of
the British National Association for Health.

Barbara Cartland

The world's bestselling author of romantic fiction. Her stories are always captivating tales of intrigue, adventure and love.